Voices from the Mountain

Novels by Hal Burton

Cave of Secrets

The Penny Red Enigma

Voices from the Mountain

Hal Burton

Voices from the Mountain

Copyright © 2006 by Hal Burton

All rights reserved. No part of this book may be used or reproduced, in any form, without permission of the copyright owner.

All characters in this book are fictitious and any resemblance to actual persons, living or dead, is purely coincidental.

Printed and bound by Gorham Printing
   Rochester, Washington

Published by Hal Burton Publishing
   Lilliwaup, Washington

First Edition, First Printing – March 2006

Map on page 148, © 1984 from *Olympic Mountain Trail Guide,* 2nd Edition by Robert L. Wood, reprinted with permission of the publisher, The Mountaineers, Seattle, Washington.

Cave and Anderson Pass descent photos -- Hal Burton

Author's photo – by Jeanette Burton

Cover design by Jeanette Burton

Library of Congress Control Number: 2005911343

ISBN – 0-9725707-8-0

Acknowledgements

As with my two previous novels, there are many people to thank for their help in the telling of this tale.

During the course of writing, I participated in three writer's groups and members of each kept me on the straight and narrow, both for story content and punctuation. Especially supportive were the folks in the Writers Roundtable that meets at Barnes & Noble in Olympia Washington.

What would we do without editors? Thanks to Debbie Simmons who read the first draft, to Jerry Horstman for his insights and editorial comments, and lastly, special kudos go to Linda Steffen, my diligent and invaluable editor.

Two books I found useful as background when writing about wilderness survival were the *Olympic National Park Nature Guide* by Larry and Nancy Eipert and *My Side of the Mountain* by Jean Craighead George. The latter would be especially educational and entertaining to any young people planning a trip into the backcountry.

Finally, nothing would be accomplished and completed without the support and encouragement of my wife, Jeanette.

Who They Are

Ray Wellsford - University Student
Pete Fairchild – University Student – Friend of Ray Wellsford
Larry Perkins – University Student – Friend of Ray Wellsford
Gordy Shandy – University Student – Friend of Ray Wellsford
Hank Mason – University Student – Class President
Al Stoker – Freshman Student – Fraternity Pledge

Jules Schlossburg – Seattle Psychologist
Dave Casper – Seattle Police Detective
Donna Jones – University Student
Brian Zerbeck – University Student

Bill O'Hara – Viet Nam Vet – Recluse
Angela Rhodes – Summer Ranger – College Student
Edie Cox – Owner, Amanda Park Mercantile
Lan Thi – Vietnamese Immigrant

Ben Maxwell – Clallam County Sheriff
Dick Wilcox – Jefferson County Sheriff
Kyle Peterson – Deputy Sheriff – Jefferson County

Prologue

Session by the Bay
September 1980

Dr. Schlossburg didn't pull out the crystal pendant, which perhaps signaled something new for our session.

"I want you to start today by telling me about the two most important events in your life. The best and the worst."

It was my third sitting with Dr. Jules Schlossburg, and as usual in our morning meetings, he spent the first minutes seated across from me in his red leather chair, silently drinking his coffee and looking out at the ships in Elliot Bay. I think he believed it made me relax to sit and say nothing. At first it had the opposite effect and I babbled incessantly. Now, getting used to the routine, I too sat pensively, sipping coffee and waiting for his lead.

"You mean recently?" I said, thinking that at least one event should be obvious by now.

"No. In your whole life." He reached for one of his briar pipes.

"You mean in my two lives?"

"If you wish."

There was little doubt in my mind what events I would select.

"The best would have to be discovering who I really am."

"And the worst?" Schlossburg asked. He jotted something on the pad on his desk, replaced an unlit pipe in its stand and swiveled his chair to gaze out the window while he waited for my answer.

"That would have to be when I realized one of my friends tried to kill me."

"Was that when you returned to Mt. Anderson Pass?"

"Yes."

"Did you start to remember more of your past then?"

"Yes. Recollections just came rushing back. In my head I heard voices, just like the mountains were talking to me."

"Voices, that's interesting." His expression was unchanged when he again faced forward.

Schlossburg made some more notes and for one of the few times, looked directly at me. "That's when you started trying to unravel the mystery?"

"Yes, and it's been an experience I wish I hadn't had to endure."

Schlossburg set down his pen and rose. "Just remember something I learned a long time ago."

"What's that?"

"When bad things happen you should keep the lesson, but throw away the experience."

Brotherhood Eternal

Spider web-like coverings of English Ivy spread over the red brick facades of many of the fraternity houses along "Greek Row." Freshly painted forest green shutters, steep shake shingled roofs and whitewashed dormers usually completed the backdrop scene for the annual picture of the Chapter members that would appear in the fraternity's semi-annual newsletter. Much like the adage about the cover of a book, however, life inside a college campus fraternity house bore little resemblance to how large, well maintained or beautifully landscaped the exterior.

    The core nature of its members, not the number of "jocks" or Phi Beta Kappa keys members earned, was the true measure of a "good" House. Each fraternity house had its own group ethos and temperament and it was the members, especially the incoming freshman, who year in and year out set the course for the future. Occasionally an incoming class had a bad seed, a young man who outwardly is "Mr. Nice Guy," the ideal pledge, the born leader; but sublimated are serious psychological problems that negatively impact the House. In rare cases, that young man's thwarted personality leads to violent behavior.

Such was the case at Xi Beta Alpha Fraternity in the Spring of 1978.

The Xi Beta Alpha House was on 17th Avenue, just three blocks from 45th Street, and near the north entrance to the campus of the University of Washington. Originally built in 1924 and remodeled several times, the three stories and a basement provided sleeping space for forty-six resident members, ample space when non-resident active members or alumni came for dinner, weekly Chapter meetings, exchanges with sororities, or dances.

Ray Wellsford's freshman year at the U had been a mixed bag. He had enjoyed living in the Xi Alpha frat House, rowing, getting to know his "brothers" and best of all, meeting lots of girls. The downside was that he'd barely scraped by with a C-minus average and Hell Week was, as advertised, pure hell.

He had good relationships with all House members, but his closest friends were in his pledge class, in particular Gordy Shandy, Pete Fairchild and Larry Perkins. They all seemed to be in the same boat, as far as their freshman year grades. Pete ended up flunking two classes, Larry, one, and Gordy barely squeezed out a C average. The four of them stuck together, however, through some of the nastiest things that the sophomore class had done to them last spring. Now, in May of 1978, and doing much better in the grade department, they were looking forward to adding their unique slant on the initiation when the new class of freshman pledges endured their rites of passage.

Pete and Ray pledged Xi Alpha the same day and although they were physical opposites and had very different interests, they became closer friends during "Rush."

Where Ray was tall, nearly six feet two; Pete was short, barely five feet five. Pete was redheaded, light skinned, with freckles bridging an aquiline nose.

Ray had jet-black hair, eyes the color of onyx and dark olive skin, unblemished except for a scar on his upper lip left from a childhood teeter-totter mishap. His good looks were like a magnet for young coeds.

Except for freshman sorority exchanges, Pete spent most weekends dateless. They had one thing in common, though.

Both "turned out" for the rowing crew. Pete for coxswain and Ray for the eight-man freshman shell. That commonality ended, however, when their poor grades forced them both to drop the very time-demanding sport.

Larry Perkins was from Yakima and was "rushed" hard by several of the "jock" fraternity houses on campus. Xi Alpha only had one member on the football team and when Larry, who lettered in both football and basketball at East Yakima High, picked Xi Alpha as one of the fraternities to visit during Rush Week, the rush chairman made him a priority candidate. Senior, Brian Zerbeck, a starting guard and the lone football letterman in the house, also was from Yakima, and helped sway the decision. Where Pete was small and slightly built, and Ray tall, Larry was just under six feet, weighed easily 250 pounds, and had the face of an English bulldog.

Then there was Gordon Shandy. Grade-wise, the smartest of the four, Gordy was "unsmooth," as the saying went. His curly brown hair hung in unruly clumps that failed to hide his pockmarked face. Horn-rimmed glasses added to the picture of a serious academic type.

Gordy's parents had been unusually strict during his four years at Spokane High School. No drinking or smoking, no driver's license until he was eighteen, and an early curfew had made it almost impossible for Gordy to date.

Even an occasional taste of his dad's beer was forbidden. Gordy had followed all the rules. When he left Spokane for the University, the bindings came off. He was like a puppy unleashed.

It was as if his parents said, "Okay, you're on your own now so do whatever you want." There didn't seem to be a time when Gordy wasn't drunk. He threw up on one of his exchange dates, started smoking two packs of Winstons a day and came close to falling off the third floor balcony on more than one occasion. He broke two sets of his eyeglasses during Winter Quarter in two separate fights at a University District tavern. Somehow, he made it through his freshman year, tapered off on his drinking and stopped trying to "put the make" on every girl he dated.

The rest of the pledge class and most of the fraternity members called the four of them, "The Motley Crew." Maybe it was their dissimilarity that attracted them to each other, but whatever, after one year, they were inseparable friends.

Ray wasn't much for the physical abuse that often happened during Hell Week and against the advice of his brothers, openly supported the effort by the University administration to prohibit Hell Week. The feelings of his sophomore classmates in the Xi Alpha House, especially the Motley Crew, and on Greek Row in general, were a mixed bag. Most of the sophomores felt like they'd endured and now it was their turn, and the upper classmen thought it would break tradition to end it. A few, like Ray, however, thought it was time to stop.

Ray recalled how some of the high jinks in the Xi Beta Alpha House started well before spring break.

At Christmas time, his freshman class had been told that it was their responsibility to get the tree for the frat House, but at no expense to the fraternity. Also, they were expected to get a larger, taller tree than the record size of the previous class. Of course, they never were told the measurement before they departed. Thinking back on that escapade for his class, made Ray realize how stupid and risky it had been.

Hank Mason, the class president, had scoped out several potential sources, but eventually settled on Mike's, a tree sale lot near 50th Street, on Aurora Avenue. They drove to the lot after midnight. Ray and Gordy acted as lookouts while the rest used their flashlights to select the biggest fir they could spot. Getting it into Cloyd Carson's old Chevy trunk proved to be no easy task. For what seemed to Ray like fifteen to twenty minutes, though actually was only five, the sixteen pledges tied down the tree, climbed back in their cars and headed south down the alley behind Mike's, to 45th Street, and back to the fraternity House.

Ray had known Pete Fairchild from their Boy Scout days at Camp Parsons on Hood Canal and was happy when they both pledged Xi Alpha. They'd double-dated once in their freshman year and up to recently, had been dating girls from the Theta House. Pete had gone to Roosevelt High School. Pete also became a good friend of Hank's, and Ray remembered the two of them proudly dragging the purloined Christmas tree into the House.

Of course, they were promptly told that their tree was well below the size provided by the previous class, though never substantiated with any real numbers. Brian Zerbeck was especially vocal and announced that he would be delivering an extra paddle to each pledge during Hell Week. And so it went. As Sophomores, Ray and his class had followed tradition, just like the eighty-one classes before them.

Hal Burton

Pete came up with the idea of the hike on the Tuesday before Hell Week and initiation ceremonies for the freshman class. Ray immediately took to the idea and after some cajoling Gordy and Larry signed on, too. It would, "be a blast." They'd leave the week after classes were out and before anyone had to start working at summer jobs. Their sophomore class was hosting a dance and party at the House the Friday of finals week and they all had dates, even Gordy, who according to Larry, had really "shaped up." At first they thought about leaving for the hike on the Saturday after the dance, but decided one day of rest would be needed, so Sunday it was.

While most of their class focused on finals, Hell Week and the big dance, Ray and Pete spent all their extra time planning the hike in the Olympic National Park. It would take them west, up the Dosewallips River Trail, south over Mt. Anderson Pass, through Enchanted Valley, following the Quinault River, and finally, to Graves Creek Campground, near Lake Quinault on the southwest side of the Park.

Ray called his folks to tell them he'd be home to get his backpacking gear. Tom and Janice Wellsford had lived on Queen Anne Hill since Ray was four years old. Tom was a foreman at the Boeing Company's plant on East Marginal Way and Janice was the school nurse at Queen Anne High School, from where Ray had graduated. Ray didn't have any siblings, but unlike most of his friends, he did have two loving parents. Pete's mom had died when he was ten, Larry's dad had been killed in Viet Nam and Gordy's parents got divorced midway through his freshman year at the University.

Hank Mason's mom was remarried, but Pete told Ray that Hank's stepfather had a serious drinking problem and was currently serving time at the prison in Clallam Bay.

When Ray returned to the frat House he and Pete put the finishing touches on their plans for the hike and then joined their fraternity brothers in preparing for Hell Week, freshman class initiation and the Spring Dance.

The Fraternity House

Party Time

As with most social functions held at the Xi Alpha House, the living room was converted to a dance floor and the dining hall tables were arranged to serve drinks and snacks.

For special events, like the Spring Dance, the Library/Study room on the main floor was also cleared to make room for dancing, as there were usually more than forty couples. The larger of the two downstairs bathrooms was transformed into a powder room for the girls. The rest of the House was officially off-limits to any female guests. This restriction included the House member's second floor rooms and especially the third floor sleeping area.

Two kegs of Olympia beer were temporarily stored under the back stairs. As usual, Bob Johnson, the House cook, signed for them, and he would help tap them before he left for the day, at seven.

Voices from the Mountain

Ray started down the front circular stairway with an armload of 45's, when he met Pete coming up.

"I thought you already took off," Ray said.

"I did, but I forgot the corsage. How about you? You're running late."

"No. Jane stayed overnight at the Theta House, so there's no hurry."

"This is your third or fourth date with her, isn't it?" Pete asked, continuing to talk as he reached the second floor.

"Third. How about you, I haven't met this one yet, have I?"

Pete and Gordy were each bringing girls they'd only dated twice. Larry had been going steady with his date, Karen Simpson, for about a year.

"No, you haven't. Okay, see you later," said Pete, as he disappeared down the hallway.

Ray continued down the stairs and headed for the living room to add his 45's to the stack of records that would be played for the dance. Freshman Al Stoker was in charge of the music for the night, and he was getting the House's stereo set up when Ray entered.

"Here's my contribution, Al."

"Thanks. You haven't seen Larry have you?" Al asked. "He's supposed to bring some records, too."

"No. I think he left about an hour ago to get Karen."

Ray turned to leave and just caught a glimpse of Gordy and Pete going out the front door. *Guess I'd better head for the Theta House and get Jane*, he thought.

Ray and Jane, Larry and Karen, Pete and his date Betty Fowler, and Gordy and his date Joanne Mitchell initially sat off by themselves. As the evening wore on, they mixed in with everyone and exchanged partners on the packed dance floor, which for Ray was something he preferred not doing.

When someone started a Congo line, Ray took the opportunity to slip away and get a fresh glass of beer.

Ray was worried about Gordy. Gordy had cut back substantially on his drinking since their freshman year, but tonight he seemed to be reverting to kind. His date Joanne seemed to be equally tipsy and the two of them were bumping into everyone on the dance floor. Just as Ray was about to say something to them, Gordy and Joanne left the Congo line and informed everyone in earshot that they were going outside for a breath of fresh air. He winked slyly at Ray as he passed by, his arm wrapped around Joanne, his hand cupped over her rear.

Ray hadn't seen Pete and Betty Fowler in a while and when Jane went to the powder room with Karen, he asked Larry if he'd seen them. He hadn't.

Then Ray spotted Hank drawing another beer from the keg.

"More beer will make you sweat extra, Hank." It was the House joke, especially among engineering majors, that Hank's body odor increased exponentially with each glass of beer.

"This is only my third," he offered, indignantly.

Ray shrugged his shoulders as if to say, okay, it's your funeral. "By the way, have you seen Pete?"

"I saw Betty and him about a half hour ago getting some beer. Not since then. Refill?" his words becoming slurred.

"No, thanks, I'm fine. I'll just wait here for Jane," Ray said.

"Okay, if I see Pete, I'll tell him you're looking for him."

Abruptly the music's volume went up two fold and Ray and Hank walked over to the dance floor to see what was going on.

Several of the brothers were yelling, "Go Brian, go!"

In the center of the dance floor, Brian and his date, Donna Jones, were wildly dancing to the Bee Gees *Stay'n Alive*. By now, they'd jostled most of the other couples out of the way.

Brian was no John Travolta and Donna was having trouble dancing, while at the same time keeping her ample bosom from popping out of her very low-cut dress. Soon, all the men on and off the dance floor were ogling her and, Ray thought, all wishing for the fallout to occur.

It didn't, and Brian, with Donna in tow, left the dance floor and collapsed in the leather couch by the window when Al started playing a slow dance tune from a Chicago album.

Jane still wasn't back, so Ray decided to heed his kidney's call for relief and headed upstairs to the second floor bathroom. As he passed Pete's room he heard giggling of a very obvious female quality. *So this is where Pete's been. Naughty, naughty.* But then, this was typical of Pete. He had always tried to make up for his small stature with bravado and an overactive drive for conquest of the opposite sex. Ray ignored the sounds and thought it likely Pete wasn't the only brother violating one of the House rules this night. He, himself, had almost "gone all the way" with Carol Thumer on the third floor, during Winter Break.

At ten-thirty, Al Stoker took a respite from his DJ role and most everyone went outside for a smoke or down to the basement to play pool or ping-pong. Jane and Karen went to the powder room again, Larry went for a smoke, and Ray decided it was time to see if Pete had come up for air. As he neared Pete's room, he heard a door at the end of the hallway slam shut. Looking in that direction, he caught sight of a guy turning the corner, and heard the sound of his shoes pounding down the back stairs. He couldn't tell for sure who it was, but whomever; he had briefly turned to glance in Ray's direction.

As Ray approached Pete's door, about half way down the hallway, he heard muffled cries. At first he thought they were coming from Pete's room, but the cries definitely were further away, past the bathroom, and they grew louder as he neared the back stairs.

The room at the end of the dimly lit hallway was used for storage and it was from this room that the crying sounds came. He tried the door, but it only opened slightly, blocked by something unseen.

Now the sounds were more whimpers than cries. He knocked on the door.

"Hey in there!" Still no response, but then he heard the sound of movement and sobbing.

"Please get my friend Sharon for me."

The door opened enough so Ray could make out the girl's face.

"You're Donna, right. Brian's date?"

"Yes, but please get Sharon for me. Sharon Franklin. She's with Todd Jensen."

"Okay, but can't you come out?"

"No, I'm, ah, hurt and …" she said hesitantly.

Donna opened the door a little wider and Ray could see that her face was bruised; her hair disheveled and there was what looked like blood on her lip.

"Let me help you."

"No … please, just get Sharon for me."

"All right, I'll be right back."

He turned the corner and quickly went down the back stairs.

―――

The rest of the night was chaotic.

Sharon Franklin and Ray's girlfriend, Jane, helped Donna to the bathroom on the second floor. Jane told Ray what had happened to Donna and then asked him to tell Duane Rogers, the Chapter president.

Whether it was Duane or someone else that called didn't matter, but within what seemed like just a few minutes, both the University of Washington Campus Police, the Seattle Police Department and an Emergency Aid car arrived at the Xi Beta Alpha Fraternity House.

Then the questioning began and they learned what had happened to Donna.

She had been pulled into the utility closet and raped! It became obvious from the questioning that Donna had not seen her attacker's face. As Ray was to learn, Donna, impatient to use the overcrowded first floor powder room, got out of line and took the back stairs to the second floor to use the mens. She heard someone behind her, but before she could turn to see who it was, the attacker grabbed her around the neck and pushed her into the utility room.

Her attacker said little as he forced her into a corner, pushed up her dress and struggled to pull down her panties with his free hand. He swore and hit her hard on the back of the head when she resisted. Gaining control, he roughly thrust himself into her. Frustrated when he went prematurely flaccid, he hit her again and after calling her a slut, left Donna curled up on the floor of the small, dark room.

During Ray's questioning session, he told the Seattle Police Department of the person he fleetingly saw at the end of the hallway, but because of the distance and poor lighting, he could not identify him. He couldn't even say for sure whether the person was tall or short, light-skinned, or dark. He did remember that the person turned his head slightly and glanced in Ray's direction, before descending the stairs.

"So, he definitely saw you?" Sergeant Dave Casper asked.

"Yes."

"But you didn't see his face and he didn't seem familiar?"

"No. As I said, it was dark at that end of the hall," Ray said in frustration.

By midnight the police finished questioning the fraternity members and their dates. Duane gave the police a list of the members and guests that had either departed the dance before the time of the attack, left before the police arrived, or in the case of some members, had not attended the dance. Donna was briefly questioned and then taken to University Hospital.

The next day, Sergeant Casper, of the Seattle Police Department, and Lieutenant Billings of the Campus Police, questioned Donna at her home in the Wallingford district. Two years later, Casper would recall the meeting.

"And you're sure you can't say whether he was tall, medium height, thin, or heavy?"

"No," Donna answered. "It was dark and it all happened so fast."

"He never spoke?"

"A couple of times. He swore, when he had trouble with my panties. That's when he hit me the first time."

"Did he say anything else?"

"Called me a dirty slut." She hesitated. "Then he said either little bitch or witch ...I'm not sure."

"You'd been drinking heavily, several people have told us," Billings said.

"Also, some of the girls we interviewed said you were putting on quite a show on the dance floor," Casper added. "Maybe you flirted just a little too much."

"And you're sure you can't remember anything else about him?" Billings interjected.

"He did smell of cigarettes, and oh yes, he was wearing cologne, the musk smelling kind."

Ray was questioned again the next day, but could add no additional information. When he was told about being available for further questioning, he mentioned the hike he, Gordon, Pete and Larry were taking. Apparently Pete had mentioned it too, and Sergeant Casper told Ray that it would be okay, but to check in when they returned. Still, Ray felt maybe they should reschedule, but in the end Larry and Pete convinced him that they should go ahead. Hank Mason volunteered to drive them to the Dosewallips Ranger Station in Larry's car and then three days later, pick them up at Graves Creek Campground. Hank was from nearby Forks and said he needed a way home anyway, so it wasn't a really hard sell.

The day before they left, the *Seattle Post Intelligencer* ran a follow-up story about the attack at Xi Beta. It reported the police had no new clues to the identity of the assailant, but Sgt. Casper was quoted as saying they were continuing the investigation and the perpetrator, when caught, would be charged with felony assault and rape.

That same day, Ray took a hike around the campus and in the evening he was nursing blisters on both feet. He'd obviously waited too long to break in his new *Danners*. The *Danner* boots were his pride and joy and he borrowed Hank's leather burning set to add his initials to both boots.

Hank was packing when Ray returned the burning set.

"Thanks for driving us, Hank."

"No problem. I almost wish I was going with you guys, but I'd have to get in better shape. I've done some hiking, you know, a couple of times in Tull Canyon, but mostly in the Hoh River Valley."

"Tull Canyon. Isn't that where the B-17 crashed years ago?"

"Yeah, in 1952, and parts of the wreckage are all over the place."

"Interesting. Listen, Hank, we really need a driver, so maybe next time."

"That's fine. I understand. Heard anything more about the rape?"

"Not really. I'm supposed to get with the police when we get back, though. Maybe try hypnosis."

"Hypnosis, wow."

Ray turned to go. "Thanks again for the burning set. I'd better get my packing done too."

Hank smiled and nodded. "Okay, see you guys in the morning."

Olympic Trek

The trail narrowed as it wove between a colonnade of moss-laden trees and ancient decaying stumps covered with a variety of colorful shelf fungi. As they continued climbing, roots across the path demanded keeping their eyes lowered to the way. Grooved and polished rocks protruded everywhere, so that it seemed like they were walking on an old cobblestone street, but one crisscrossed with tree limbs.

Pete stumbled over some entwined roots, obscured by a clump of deer ferns, and almost went down.

"Watch out," he yelled, catching his balance.

Ray and Larry had twice hiked the West Fork Dosewallips River Trail as far as Honeymoon Meadows Campground. Pete and Ray hiked from Graves Creek to the Chalet in Enchanted

Valley. Gordy had been on several hikes in northern Idaho and once hiked the Wagonwheel Lake Trail, near Lake Cushman. None of the four had ever traversed the Park from the east to the west.

Larry got them to the trailhead about an hour later than they'd planned. The gravel road from Brinnon to the Dosewallips Campground was narrow, filled with chuckholes, dusty and mostly uphill. It reminded Gordy of most of the rural roads around Spokane, only they were flat, not climbing steadily from sea level to 1600 foot elevation.

They'd divided up the gear and food the previous night, so after handing over the car keys to Hank Mason and registering with the Park Ranger, they set off for their first stop of the day, Dose Forks. It was a great day for hiking, about seventy degrees, clear, and to their delight, no one else had registered earlier, so they should have the trail to themselves, at least for a while. Pete led the way, followed by Ray, then Gordy and bringing up the rear, Larry.

Because of the late start, Ray was concerned whether they would get to Diamond Meadows before nightfall. Though it was mid summer and stayed light until after nine, the tall cedar and firs and high cliffs of the mountain terrain often obscured the sun. Ray remembered one time two summers ago when he set up camp on Lena Lake around six and by seven it was dark.

Ray avoided the tree root that had tripped Pete, and yelled a word of warning back to Gordy and Larry. Pete slowed his pace, now more vigilant.

"I see what you mean about a steady uphill grind," said Pete, quickly looking over his shoulder at Ray, whose face was almost hidden by his large and floppy, Australian-style hat.

"It isn't too bad for a while. Remember, we only climb a few hundred feet before we get to Dose Forks," Ray responded.

"That's when the fun begins," hollered Larry from the rear.

Soon they left the protective canopy of trees and started to ascend a steep hillside covered with alpine flowers. Lupines, Indian Paintbrush, thistles and daisies were thick on either side of the trail and glistened in the morning sunlight.

"Let's stop," said Gordy, "I've got to shed this jacket."

"Time for a break, anyway," said Ray, "but let's wait until we're back in some shade."

When they reached the top of the hill, the trail leveled off and stately cedars, firs and hemlocks once again enclosed them and provided a welcome screen from the sun.

"Okay, let's stop here," said Ray, gesturing to a clearing surrounded by fallen trees that would provide good support for their heavy packs.

After a brief rest, they donned their packs and set out once more, this time with Gordy in the lead. Soon they emerged from the thick tree stands, but this time, instead of climbing, the trail led down to a log bridge. An old wooden sign said, "Hungry Creek."

"Hold up for a minute, Gordy, I want to check the map," Ray said, reaching the other side of the bridge.

Larry followed Ray. "How much longer?"

"Looks like about three miles to Diamond Meadows," Ray said. He folded the *Green Trails* map and returned it to the side pocket of his pack. "We're not too far from Big Timber Camp, then we head down again for a while, before we climb to Diamond Meadows. We should be there about four."

Most of the trail-talk consisted of griping about their heavy packs and how hot it was. Pete twice thought he saw someone on the trail behind him, but no one passed when they stopped. Not a soul brought up the subject of the rape. It was as if it had happened in another world; perhaps another time.

When they stopped for lunch at Big Timber, though, Pete broke the ice. "No one's said anything about the other night."

"What do you mean, Pete?" said Gordy.

"Damn, quit being so mealy-mouthed, Gordy. It's got to be on all our minds," Pete said. "The attack at the party, all the questioning, and the truth that one of our brothers probably did it." Gordy shrugged his shoulders.

"I know. I just wish it would go away. Sorry, Pete."

"Okay, you guys," said Larry, "let's save it for another time." He looked scornfully at Pete, then Gordy.

"Pete, Larry's right, let's drop it for now. Maybe tonight at Diamond Meadows we can talk about it," Ray said. "Come on, Elk Lick Creek is just two miles ahead."

The log bridge across Elk Lick Creek was narrow and well-worn; the bridge handrail, thin and bowed. Ray stepped aside to let them pass as he took another look at his map before carefully traversing.

"It should be just another half-mile," he said, as he joined them.

The trail headed upwards again and just when they thought the steady grind of switchbacks would not stop, they broke out of the tree cover to enter a large clearing, right at the edge of the river.

"We're here!" shouted Pete.

No other backpackers were there so they had their choice of the ten sites. Gordy dropped his pack at the site nearest the river; one that had a fire pit with logs circling it. "This should do," he announced, not really asking for their agreement. The ground was reasonably level and free of any large roots or rocks, however, so they silently agreed and dropped their packs next to Gordy's.

Later around the campfire, Pete again brought up the subject they had all been avoiding.

"So, who do you think did it?" he asked to no one in particular.

"I don't have a clue," said Larry, "Ray's the only one who may have gotten a look at the guy."

"A quick peek is more like it, and it was dark," said Ray.

"Are you supposed to talk to the cops again?" asked Gordy.

"Maybe. They asked my parents about putting me under hypnosis to see if I could remember anything more." He yawned. "You know, I'm ready for the sack."

"Me too," said Pete. "It's only seven-thirty, but I'm beat."

The aroma of brewing coffee floated across the campsite and into their tent. Ray unzipped his sleeping bag and raised himself just enough to look out the screened entry flap. Gordy had the fire going and was mixing something in one of their cooking pots. Ray glanced down and found that he was not the only one still "in the sack." Pete and Larry were both burrowed deeply in their down bags. He looked at his watch, the hands just visible in the morning light. *Five* o'clock, *cry'n out loud*, he thought, *might as well get up*. He was hurting anyway and wishing he'd brought a thicker ground mat. Besides he needed to relieve himself and the coffee smell was very enticing. He scooted up enough to get his legs out, reached above his head and retrieved his jeans. Gordy must have heard his movement.

"Come on guys, time to rise and shine! As my dad's drill sergeant used to holler at reveille, 'Drop your cocks and grab your socks'."

Ray pulled on his shirt, grabbed his boots and unzipped the tent flap. "Come on Pete, Larry, time to get up, before Gordy remembers some more pithy sayings." They both stirred and grunted assent. Pete added a choice word or two as Ray left the tent.

"What's for breakfast?"

"You should know, Ray, you made up the menu."

"Looks like pancake mix to me, Gordy. I'll be right back, and then I'll help. Coffee smells great," said Ray, walking in the direction of the one pit toilet at the campsite.

The choice of "toilets" in the backcountry was limited. Most developed campsites had one or two at most and often the stench and flies were so bad that a nearby log or clump of trees was a preferred alternative. The lone outhouse at Diamond Meadows wasn't too bad, but Ray didn't overstay his welcome. Pete was heading his way.

"Good morning, Pete, you'll love the aroma."

"Jeez, it's hardly daylight, damn that ground was hard!"

―――※―――

By seven-thirty they finished breakfast, washed up the utensils, packed up, filled the canteens and cleaned the campsite. They knew it would be a grueling day, mostly climbing all morning until they reached Anderson Pass and started their long descent alongside the Quinault River.

It was more than they'd bargained for. The first creek they crossed was missing its log bridge, so they had to climb down to the creek level, cross by using rocks that barely broke the surface and scramble up the other side to rejoin the trail.

The second creek was no better and Larry slipped during the crossing, remaining upright, but filling his boots with the cold water. It took them over three hours to reach Honeymoon Meadows, where they took a much-needed rest.

"How far up did we climb?" asked Larry.

"About a thousand feet," said Ray. "It felt like a lot more."

"You'd better change your socks, Larry," said Gordy.

After crossing the river and leaving the Honeymoon Meadows campsite, they entered a wide valley covered with knee-high sword ferns, bull thistles and bear grass. The plants and blades of grass were so thick the path was barely visible.

"From a distance, it almost looks a lot like the early wheat fields around home," Larry said.

"You can see why they called it a meadow," said Pete, nodding.

"Yeah, but look, it starts to climb pretty soon. You can see ahead where it goes up the hillside," Gordy said. Gordy was in the lead and just as he finished his observation, down he went. "Shit!"

They didn't hear anything else as they rushed to him. Gordy was barely visible above the thick grass. Then, "Crap! I can't get up."

Gordy's boot was wedged under a root, but his well-stuffed backpack cushioned his fall. Once they removed his pack he could at least sit up. Then, carefully he turned his boot and pulled his right leg free of the tree root. "Ouch!"

Ray helped him to his feet. "Can you put any weight on it?"

"I'm standing, aren't I?" Gordy shifted his weight and flexed his leg. "It hurts a little, but I think it's just a small sprain."

"How about the rest of you?" asked Larry, who was holding Gordy's backpack.

"No, I think I'm okay. Maybe a few sore spots. Christ, I could use a cigarette right now."

"You should be glad you quit! Your pack really saved you, by the way, but I'd check it for any broken stuff," said Larry.

With his ankle wrapped in an Ace bandage from Pete's first aid kit and his pack once more on his back, Gordy led the way. As he'd earlier observed, the path ascended the hillside. At 3600 feet and now about two and a half miles from their morning starting point, they reached the junction with the trail to LaCrosse Pass. Gordy was moving slowly and doing a good imitation of deputy Chester Goode from *Gunsmoke*.

"How much farther to the Pass?" Gordy asked, frowning.

"A couple miles, maybe a little less. We should break out of this cover soon and then we'll be able to see the twin peaks of Anderson and also Mt. LaCrosse," said Pete.

"I need to rest my ankle a bit." Gordy leaned against a nearby rock and putting his weight on one leg, flexed the other.

Ray got out his map and checked his watch. He knew that at their current pace with at least another eight or nine hundred feet to climb, they'd be hard pressed to make it to the Enchanted Valley today. The five-mile downhill side from Anderson Pass would be doubly hard on all of them, but especially Gordy. He looked up from the map.

"Maybe we ought to consider staying at Anderson Pass Camp tonight?" They looked at Gordy for his reaction.

"Yeah, maybe we should," said Pete. Larry nodded.

Gordy at first argued against the idea, but it was apparent he needed the rest and when they reached Anderson Pass Camp, his limp was even more pronounced. He'd fashioned a cane out of a tree limb and if he hadn't had that, Ray doubted Gordy would have made the last hundred feet.

Like their experience at Diamond Meadows, there were no other campers at Anderson. They'd only seen one pair of hikers that day, and they said they were going to take the LaCrosse Pass Trail and head toward the Duckabush.

Gordy found a tree stump and using it to support his weight, loosened the straps and got out of his backpack.

"I'm going to soak my leg in the creek."

They'd just finished their meal and Larry and Pete were cleaning the dishes and pots at the edge of the creek. Ray and Gordy were alone.

"How's the leg?" Ray asked

"A little better. I'm glad we stopped. Sorry for the delay, Ray."

"That's okay. It's not your fault. Besides, it's beautiful here and we can take it easy tomorrow and still get to Graves Creek by nightfall."

"What about Hank. Won't he get worried when we're not there on time?"

"He may, but I told him we could be late and just to wait it out. Want some more cocoa?"

"No, thanks, if I drink any more I'll have to get up in the night and on this leg, I'd just as soon have a good, long sleep. Besides, in case you haven't noticed, there's no outhouse."

"Yes, but think of the adventure. Taking a moonlight piss in the snow at the base of Anderson Glacier." Ray smiled.

They were at 3600 feet and as no campfires were allowed in the park above 3500 feet, the nearby snow quickly cooled the air as the sun fell below the treetops and dropped out of sight. Ray pulled his new *Pacific Trail* jacket tightly around himself.

"We need to get an early start, so I'm turning in soon," said Ray to Pete and Larry as they approached. Gordy's already in the tent. I'm going to take a walk. I'll be right back"

"Alright, we'll be there shortly. Just going to put some of the gear away," Pete said. "Be careful, there's quite a drop-off above that moraine and several patches of snow near the edge."

"Remember to hang your food up too," added Larry, "we saw some big tracks down by the creek."

Somewhere around one, Ray wished he'd not had that last cup of cocoa. He had joked about an "adventure," but really didn't relish the idea of climbing out of the tent and finding a spot to relieve himself. He slipped on his pants and coat. He'd left his heavy wool socks on, but decided to pull on his boots. It would be plenty cold at their altitude. As he exited the tent, he sensed movement behind him and hoped he hadn't woken anyone.

He'd been waiting for an opportunity for two days. Ray seemed never to be alone. Now, almost to the point of giving up, opportunity had finally presented itself. Cautiously, he moved forward.

The moon was partially obscured and Ray berated himself for forgetting to bring a flashlight. As he made his way to the perimeter of the campsite, he heard a twig snap behind him. *What the hell!* He turned, not really afraid, but puzzled.

"Gordy, Larry, Pete?"

No one answered. The only sound was the splashing river water, fainter now. He took several more steps, going further away from the water and remembering Pete's admonition as he neared the edge. *It really does drop off here*, he thought, as he unzipped his fly. Just then he heard what sounded like leaves rustling, and turned again. He couldn't tell for sure who or what it was. *Maybe an animal*, he thought, *or the wind*. Something scurried through the nearby brush. *A raccoon looking for food? At this elevation, not likely.*

Now he was really mystified. *Maybe a bobcat?* No noise now.

His tension lessened, but shortly increased when he heard what sounded like a large tree branch snapping. He felt a surge of adrenaline. *A bear? Another camper?*

Instinctively he held his breath.

"Guys? Come on. Who's there?"

A human shape emerged from behind a nearby tree, the moonlight framing its shadow.

"I thought I heard someone. Is that you Pete? Came to join me, huh?"

Still no answer. "Come on Larry, Gordy, you guys had me scared for a minute."

Ray turned back to his task. "Okay, joke's over. Watch your step, it's a long way down."

The blow to his head came swift and hard and Ray literally flew off the edge. Down, down, into the black void. Silence.

"Sorry 'bout that, Ray," he said quietly, and crept back into the dark.

Hal Burton

Enchanted Valley Chalet

Olympic National Park

The Mountain Man

Many claim to have caught glimpses of a mountain man trudging through the rain forests of the Olympic National Park. Some backpackers were convinced that he had been in their campsites when food mysteriously disappeared. In 1977, one hiker swore he'd seen the shadow of a huge man outside his tent and the next morning, found giant footprints leaving the campsite. In the spring of 1978, a Park Ranger, concerned as to who was hiking in an area prone to avalanches, followed a set of snowshoe tracks until they disappeared at the edge of Anderson Glacier. Residents of rural Jefferson County continued to report missing chickens and eggs. Several farmers told of seeing a large fur-covered animal running upright out of their barns, but in all, the existence of a mountain man was assumed by most to be just a myth. Like the tales of Bigfoot and Sasquatch, reports of sightings were fine fodder, adding local color for the benefit of tourists, and for telling scary stories around Boy Scout campfires. The sightings continued, however, and when clothing was stolen from the Lake Quinault Lodge maintenance building, many were convinced it had been the work of the elusive mountain man.

Even more bewildering was that at the same time a recent sighting was reported on the east side of the park, near Upper Lena Lake, a hiker on the west side alleged to have seen the mountain man on the Hoh River Trail.

He shivered and reached out in the darkness, searching with his left hand. He touched nothing. His right arm seemed to be bound to his side and he couldn't move his legs. Using his left arm again, he tried pushing himself up to a sitting position. Pain shot through his body.

"Don't move around, you'll tear the bandages."

Since regaining consciousness he'd sensed the presence of someone and called out several times, but no one had answered until now.

"Where am I?" he asked to the unseen voice.

"Don't worry about that, just lie still."

"Where are you? I can't see. Is it night?"

"No, afternoon. You're eyes are covered by a bandage," he said.

Reaching up he touched his face and found that his entire head was covered.

"What happened to me?"

"I don't know," the voice said. "Now rest and don't try to move again. I'm leaving for a while."

"Don't go!" Silence.

He disregarded the advice and tried again to push himself up, but like before, the pain was intense and he ceased trying. Feeling the warmth of a crackling fire, he relaxed and soon fell asleep.

Perhaps it was the smell of smoke or possibly the snapping noise of burning wood that woke him, he wasn't sure, but he knew that once more he wasn't alone.

"How long were you gone?"

"About an hour. It's getting dark and colder so I needed to get more wood for the fire."

"Where are we?"

"In a cave. Above the Valley."

"What Valley? Where? I mean ... I don't remember how I got here, or how I was injured."

"You don't remember?" he said, sounding more distant.

"Are you leaving again?"

"No, getting the rest of the wood inside. Feels like it's going to storm."

The injured man could hear the sound of thunder and felt a cool breeze. "Yes, it does sound like it. What's your name, I need to call you something."

There was no response. Then momentarily, he could hear returning footsteps.

"I heard you, I was pulling the tarp across the opening. Bill, just call me Bill. What's yours?"

And there it was. *What is my name? How did I get here? My name! My God, I don't know.*

"I don't know," the injured man answered, his voice wavering.

"You don't know?" said the unseen voice that called himself Bill.

Bill had already searched and found no identification on the young man. No wallet and nothing in his shirt or blue jean pockets. His coat was torn to pieces. The only potentially

identifying clues Bill found were two letters, "R" and "W", burned into each of his leather boots.
"Do the letters R and W mean anything?" Bill asked.
"No, should they?"
"I'll explain later, but for now, I'm going to call you RW. How's that?" Bill moved closer. "When you're feeling up to it, I need to get those clothes off. Got some here that should fit you fine. Courtesy of the folks at Lake Quinault Lodge."

Bill had found the young man he later dubbed RW lying unconscious at the top of a moraine, at the edge of Anderson Glacier, several hundred feet below Anderson Pass Campsite.

At first, he thought the man was dead, but a quick check of the young man's pulse had revealed the opposite. Bill hadn't seen any obviously broken bones, though he wasn't able to see below the knee on one leg, as it was lodged between two boulders. Either way, he needed to move him before exposure accomplished what an apparent fall had not. *How long had he been there?* Bill had thought. *Probably a day, at most, maybe only since morning. Why wasn't someone looking for him?* Huge rocks had concealed RW from anyone looking over the ledge above, but still, Bill was puzzled. The only people he'd seen in days were a Forest Service trail crew near White Creek.

Bill had looked for anything to pry apart the boulders, but he was above the tree line, so there were no branches to be found. His bow wouldn't do. *Maybe his walking stick?* The stick had broken on the first try, but putting the two pieces together and using a nearby rock as a fulcrum, he'd moved one of the boulders enough to pull the pinned leg free.

The cave had been five miles away, at the northern edge of the Enchanted Valley, near the Falls. It would be dark soon. The trail he usually took when hunting and checking his traps had been covered by snow, so he'd bypassed the snow bank by climbing down to the moraine, planning to go across and then up to the other side to reach the cliffs surrounding the glacier,

Voices from the Mountain

where he'd seen mountain goats two days previously.

Bill had managed to carry the limp body of the young man back up the steep slope to the snow covered trail, from where he had earlier made his descent. *I'll never get both of us back before dark*, he remembered thinking. RW had softly moaned.

Using the two halves of his walking stick, he'd hollowed out a refuge in the snow that would protect them through the night. He'd drawn RW close and pulled his fur coat over them. Drifting off to sleep, Bill had wondered how he would get them to his cave tomorrow. Then he remembered something he'd seen the day before. *Yes!*

His hand movements cast animated shadows on the cave wall creating an eerie aura to the scene.

"Ouch!"

"Hold still, I don't want to pull any of the skin away from around your eyes."

Bill worked slowly, trying to be as gentle as he could. He'd decided yesterday that it was time to see if his first aid had worked and how much damage, if any, there was to RW's eyes. After unwinding several wraps, he could see that the left eye was still swollen shut, but the swelling had decreased. He gently rubbed some Vaseline around RW's eye. *Time will tell on this one*, Bill thought.

"I still can't see," RW said, wincing, but saying nothing more.

"I know, your eyelids are still swollen shut, but this eye looks like it's healing well."

Bill continued to unwrap. The area around the right eye hadn't been as badly cut, but he had treated it just the same. The final wrap was off and only the patch of gauze remained.

"I can see some light!" RW exclaimed.

Bill carefully removed the gauze. "And now?"

Finally RW was able to put a face to the voice, blurry, yet features now distinguishable. Bill's deep-set hazel eyes were luminous, even in the dim light of the cave. A full beard covered much of his face, his brown hair pulled into a ponytail. He was tall, probably over six feet.

"You're younger than I imagined."

"Is that right? Hold still, I need to replace the gauze dressing on your other eye and cover it again." With practiced skill he attended to his young patient.

"That should do it. Now let's look at your arm and leg."

RW's right side had taken the brunt of what they guessed was a long fall, and he was now able to see the splint on his arm and the bandages around his thigh. He also noticed his right foot was wrapped in a bandage.

"I really am not sure about the arm. Could just be a bad sprain, but I put it in a splint just to make sure. The gash on the thigh was ugly, but it's healing, thanks to some fancy stitching by yours truly. Your foot was badly mangled and you may have a few broken bones there."

"What's that stuff?" RW asked, pointing to the dressing.

"Hemlock bark. It helps stop the bleeding."

"It stinks." RW looked up. "How long have I been here?"

"Five days now." Bill handed RW a stick, about four feet long, with a forked top. "Here, see if you can stand."

RW took the stick and with assistance, rose. He first put his weight on the left foot, but felt sharp pains as he shifted to the right. The image of Bill's once clear face became fuzzy.

"Oh, oh, think I'd better sit down."

"Okay," said Bill, "but next time let's see if we can get some of your clothes changed. I've been washing you off as much as I could. It's not just the hemlock poultice that stinks."

"I could probably change shirts now," RW said, his blurry vision now clearing.

"No, you rest for the present. I'll bet you're hungry?"

"Yes, I'm starved."

RW looked around. The cave was much larger than he had envisioned. He had the strange feeling that he'd been in a similarly large cave before.

The cave "room" contained a variety of furniture, most obviously handmade, like the bed frame, which looked to be constructed of tree branches lashed together with vines. A fire burned in a pit several feet away and the smoke rose gently upward. Next to the wall on his left, near the bed, was a bookcase made from tree logs. It overflowed with books and magazines. On top of the bookcase, a framed drawing of a young oriental woman rested against the wall.

Two rusty metal and cloth chairs, which looked like the kind you'd see at the beach, were on the opposite side. A pair of hurricane lamps hung on the back wall, one lit, casting a large shadow so RW couldn't tell if the cave went deeper. He lay on a second wooden bed. Close to him was a sawed-off tree stump where Bill had been sitting. A weathered wooden kitchen cabinet and a table, with two flickering candles, were to the right of the fire pit. Three unfinished woodcarvings, one identifiable as a large bird, and several chisels lay next to the candles. A large blue-metal coffee pot rested on one of the rocks that surrounded the fire. Bill retrieved a cup from the table, filled it and handed it to RW.

"Here's some tea I made from salmonberries. That should hold you for now." He walked to the cabinet, reached in, then turned, holding a can with a brown and blue label.

"How about some good old B & M baked beans?"

"Sure." He sipped the tea, savoring the taste.

"I'd a died for some of these when I was in Nam."

RW sat silently, warmed by the fire. He watched Bill open the can and scoop the beans into a pan he got from the cabinet. His eyelids were heavy. The cup slowly slipped from his hand.

Whether it was the unpleasant odor or the noise of metal hitting metal that roused him again, he didn't know. He opened his eye.

"Welcome back." Bill closed the blade on his knife and wiped some wood chips from his lap.

"Sorry."

"That's okay, I burnt the beans anyway. They're not too bad, though. Want some?"

"Sure." RW took the pie tin. "What time is it?"

"About nine, I'd guess. It was almost dark when I looked outside."

"You don't have a watch?"

"Nope, not much need of one."

RW nodded, ate the last bite and set the tin down. "Thanks. Not bad, and I was hungry."

"That's a good sign." Then, hesitantly, "Any memory coming back?"

"No."

"Well, tomorrow we need to get you up and walking if you're going to survive in these mountains. It will probably be another month before you can put a lot of weight on your leg."

"Then what?"

"Let's worry about that when you're ready. For now you're with me and if we can get you strong enough before the snows come, we'll see."

Survival

The beauty of the early spring carpet of yellow violets and oxalis did little to quell his growing impatience.

"No, not that way." Bill took the rope and forked stick from RW. "Tie the forked stick onto the end of the tree first, then bend it over. Here, I'll do it again."

Bill looped the end of the rope that didn't have a noose around the forked stick, then to the end of the small alder and then bending the tree over, drove the sharp ends in the ground.

"Now all that's left to do is carefully attach the straight stick with the bait to the forked one and you're all set." He handed the stick back to RW.

RW had tried twice to get the snare to hold, but each time the tree sprung back. The first time, the rope swiped him across the forearm, leaving a nasty welt.

"That's it. You've got it. Just open out the noose and lay it on the ground so it's just under the end of the stick with the bait."

"How's that?" RW asked, stepping back.

"Great. Now cover the noose with some small branches or leaves and you're done. It won't work all the time, but it's about the best for catching rabbits or marmots."

"There!" RW said with satisfaction.

"Finally," Bill said, "remember to wear your leather gloves or the little critter will smell you for sure and won't go near the bait. Let's head back, looks like rain."

As Bill predicted, it started to drizzle. By the time they crossed the river and began the climb back to the cave it had turned into a steady downpour. Not uncommon in the Enchanted Valley in April. It was an early spring and the snow had receded to about a thousand feet, and the Quinault was to overflowing. The log bridge they used was just inches above the rushing water.

Bill led the way as they reached the other side and started their ascent. "Time to put on our snowshoes," he said.

The now familiar trail was turning whiter and more slippery with each upward step.

"Snow's getting deeper, be careful," Bill called. RW was lagging behind.

"Slow down a bit. My leg's starting to hurt."

"Just another ten minutes or so, I want to get there before the snow makes the going any tougher."

"Okay." Then hesitantly, "Did they have snow like this where you were in Viet Nam?"

"Very little. Once in a while in the hills above the Drung village."

"When were you ...?"

Bill cut him off. "That's enough questions for today. Let's focus on getting back."

"But?"

"No buts. We'll talk about Viet Nam some other time."

RW knew enough to let it go, but he longed to know about Bill's past and his time in "Nam."

The next day Bill designated for the start of archery practice. He would teach RW using his Grizzly bow. If RW caught on, it would be beneficial to potentially have another provider.

For the practice target, Bill selected a large shelf fungus on a rotting tree, near the river's edge. A dirt bank behind the log would serve as a backboard from errant arrows. The previous night, Bill made RW read a book on archery and RW was impressed that the bow and arrow had been used as a weapon for 5000 years and then more for hunting during medieval times.

"Use the sight and try to keep your arm steady."

"The tension's too much, I can't hold it that long."

"No. It's just fine. Take a deep breath, sight and release."

"Like that?" The arrow missed the fungus, but this time at least hit the log, unlike the previous arrows that stuck out in a wide pattern in the bank.

"Better, much better," said Bill.

After several more near-misses, RW began to regularly hit the target, breaking off chunks of the sponge-like growth.

"That's enough for today. We won't call you Orion just yet, but I'm impressed."

Two days later, the lesson was on field dressing small game. As he had done previously, Bill had RW read about it the night before. Fortunately, for the sake of the lesson, there was a rabbit in one of the traps Bill set the previous day.

"Right. Keep cutting up to the breastbone. Hold your finger under the blade so you don't cut into the stomach or his guts."

Yuck and double yuck, RW thought to himself. He was getting blood all over his shirt and jeans and the sight of the loose coil of "guts," as Bill called them, brought him close to heaving his own.

"Okay. Now, reach inside and pull out his stomach and the intestines. Don't forget his butt hole, you don't want to eat that." Bill could sense that RW was more than a little squeamish and was laying it on thick.

"I got it!" RW said.

"Here's some grass to wipe out the inside and then we'll let him soak in the river. Good job."

As winter had approached it became obvious that RW would not be able to make it back to civilization. The closest road was fourteen miles away. Bill would surely have to accompany RW and he was not ready to take the risk of discovery. His only outside contact was Edie Cox, the owner of the Amanda Park Mercantile. Once the snows started to blanket the hillsides, there was no choice; RW would spend the winter with Bill.

It was Bill's third winter in the Olympic Mountains and he'd slowly learned how to deal with the cold and isolation. The foraging and hunting in summer and fall, plus the occasional clandestine treks to the nearest farm or ranger station, gave him the supplies for the long winter. He had to admit, however, that even though RW's presence had drained his cache, the company had been enjoyable. The dwindling food supply had precipitated the past week's trips into the Valley. Teaching RW how to hunt and trap was now a necessity, if, as he said, he was going to continue to live with Bill.

Bill hadn't really said yes or no. He knew, however, that though RW's physical body was healthy, his mind was not and until his memory returned, letting him reenter society would not be the best idea. So, for now, Bill went along with RW's plan.

On his next trip to Amanda Park, he would go to the library and read more back issues of the newspaper. Surely, something more would have been reported by now.

As part of setting up his new "home" in the cave, Bill had made four trips to Quinault and Amanda Park that first year. One time the library was having a book sale and he bought as many as he could carry. That was when he was reasonably clean-shaven and didn't look much different than many of the locals. Whenever he ventured out of the Park he brought back needed supplies and as many books as he could afford or get for free.

Two of the books were on first aid, one on home remedies and one was a medical dictionary. The latter he had consulted frequently since RW's arrival.

As best Bill could interpret, RW had what was called retrograde amnesia. In this type, the memory loss was for events prior to the injury and often the person will remember things in the distant past, but not the more recent.

There was hope, though. Bill found several references to cases where memory rushed back after some event triggered something in the brain. On the downside, there were several references to cases where past memories never returned. Unfortunately, so far, RW showed all the signs of being in the latter category. One thing for sure, his memory retention since regaining consciousness was not impaired. RW was a fast learner.

Something else one of the medical references suggested was that whenever an amnesia patient has a recollection, they should write it down. Bill gave RW a spiral notebook similar to the one he used for preliminary drawing and to sketch his carving designs.

Hal Burton

As his Seattle doctor had recommended, Bill used another notebook to write down what he could remember of his "bad" dreams about Viet Nam. A few more lines in the current one and he would add it to the towering stack.

"Nam"

The United States officially withdrew from Viet Nam on March 29, 1973. Known to only a few in the CIA, a small detachment of US Special Forces continued to advise the South Vietnamese in the Central Highlands, well into 1975.

Sgt. Michael William O'Hara had been a Green Beret in Viet Nam for three years. Before being reassigned to the Special Forces Camp in Ban Me Thuot in November 1974, he secretly worked with the Montagnards. He came to respect these mountain people who were fiercely loyal to the Americans. He especially admired the Drung tribesmen, many of whom he'd lived with for over a year in their remote mountain village above Ban Me Thout.

His small detachment was due to pull out of Ban Me Thout in April, but on March 4th all that changed when the North Vietnamese encircled the city.

On March 10th the North Vietnamese Army attacked, and in a matter of three days, the city was theirs.

Bill, as his buddies knew him, was assigned to the South Vietnamese 23rd Division. They put up a good battle initially, but were vastly outnumbered and most either surrendered or deserted by the end of the second day of fighting. Bill and his unit withdrew with the remains of the 23rd Division to Hue.

In Hue they joined up with the 21st Infantry Division, that was well dug in and ready for battle. Indecision by South Vietnam President Nguyen Van Thieu however, resulted in chaos and the eventual defeat of the South Vietnamese in the Central Highlands. Bill O'Hara and the few Green Berets that made it out alive from Hue eventually got to Da Nang, where CIA helicopters evacuated them to Saigon.

Bill's stay in Saigon was short-lived. He and four of his fellow Green Berets were on the second helicopter that left the US Embassy on April 29th. He was honorably discharged in June and returned to his native Seattle.

At twenty-seven, Bill had seen his share of the evils that man could do to his fellow man. The slaughters at the Drung village and then again in Hue would be forever in his memory. He had enlisted in 1970, a month after he graduated from the University of Washington. He figured he'd be drafted soon anyway, and decided he wanted a choice if he had to go to Viet Nam. Bill set his sights on becoming a Green Beret.

The Seattle he left in 1970 was not altogether different than the one he returned to in 1975. He had heard from some of his friends not to expect a hero's welcome. In fact, it would be better not to talk about the war, as for most, the war had ended in 1973. He wanted to forget what he'd experienced anyway, and besides, most of his missions were classified. He did attend a rally for Joe Hooper, the most decorated U.S. soldier in the war, but was shocked when he saw a group of students holding a Vietnam victory celebration in front of the Student Union Building. He'd been at the University that day to get some help finding a job. His four-year degree in Business Administration and five years in the Army had so far been of little value.

His experience as a Ranger and all the survival skills he learned from the mountain people did little to enhance his qualifications in the civilian world.

The counselors at the University Business Department gave him several good leads, but his age and lack of experience always put him far down the list of applicants. Finally he got a job at the Boeing Renton plant working on the 737 assembly line.

Bill lived alone in the Kensington Apartments in the Renton Highlands. His parents had divorced the year before he joined the Army. He was an only child. His dad died in 1973 and his mother remarried and moved to Denver just a month before he got out. His girl friend from his college years married the year after he left for Viet Nam.

Although he dated a few women from work and a gal he met in the apartment laundry room, Bill spent most of his nights alone, his only leisure pursuit, a lifetime passion for whittling. Occasionally he had a few beers with some other vets from work, but in general, he had few friends. Two of the friends from work, Charlie and Dave couldn't understand why he didn't date more. After all, Bill was tall, just under six feet, sandy hair with hazel eyes, and when he wanted to, he showed an engaging smile. *Maybe it was the hair*, Dave had said to Charlie on more than one occasion. Bill had been letting his normally curly hair grow long and it was now several inches over his collar. Bill's supervisor at work had also commented on it a few times. But it really had nothing to do with anything as mundane as hair length. Bill just didn't talk much and especially on dates, he was quiet to a fault. Dave just chalked it up to Bill being too intellectual for his own good.

The nightmares started after he began working at Boeing. They were always about that last night in the Drung village when the North Vietnamese Army had attacked and Lan Thi was killed. The North Vietnamese hated the Drung, and they took no prisoners.

When the attack began, Bill was drawing water from the well behind the village. Lan Thi had left for their hut a minute earlier with another full can.

The mortar barrage lasted five to six minutes, but it seemed like an eternity. The AK47's shredded what remained standing, and the soldiers continued firing as they charged the village. There was nothing Bill could do and he watched in horror as the marauding NVA torched everything in sight, repeatedly firing into the huts. Then it was silent, except for the crackling of the fires.

At dawn Bill crept into the charred remains of the village that had been his home. Nothing remained. Like every structure that had been, the hut he shared with Lan Thi was a pile of ashes. Bill wept for the first time in a long while.

Somehow he made his way to Hue.

The Fall of 1976 Bill decided to use his one-week of vacation to hike through the Olympic Mountains. He'd been active in Boy Scouts and gone to summer camps at Camp Parsons on Hood Canal. He fondly remembered the days spent hiking in the backcountry of the National Park. Bill couldn't think of a better place to go for some peace and quiet. Maybe he'd even be able to sleep through the night.

His last year at Camp Parsons, Bill, six other scouts and their section leader climbed Mt. Anderson. It was the best trip he'd ever taken in the backcountry, so he now selected the area around Mt. Anderson as his destination.

On his last day, he decided to follow one of the creeks to the falls below Chimney Peak. It was while climbing on the rocks near the falls that he discovered the cave.

He finished the entry and laid down the journal.

"Who or what's Lan Ti?"

Bill was caught off guard by RW's question. "What! Where'd you hear that name?"

"From you. You say the name when you're having one of your nightmares, which has been just about every night lately."

"It's the name of a girl and it's pronounced Thi, not Ti, and Lan, as in lawn mower."

"Well its sounds like Ti when you mumble it. So, who is she?"

Bill was silent. Then, "She's dead."

"In Viet Nam?"

"Yes."

Like the day before, whenever RW broached the subject of Bill's tour in "Nam," as he called it, Bill always found a way to change the subject.

It was the morning after their return from setting traps in the valley. Bill had an unusually bad session that kept RW awake most of the night.

"You had a really tough time last night. You hollered out several times."

"Probably because you asked me too many damn questions."

"Well at least you remember your past!" RW said. "So tell me about Lan Thi," pronouncing her name correctly this time.

Bill filled his coffee cup and surprised RW.

"Okay, and by the way, her given name, Lan, means orchid flower in Vietnamese."

Bill told of his early days in Viet Nam, his assignment to work with the Montagnards, and about his year with the Drung tribe. Finally he told RW about Lan Thi.

"She was only nineteen, probably close to your age and as fierce a fighter as any of the village males. Her father was a village elder." As he continued his voice softened and RW could also hear the pain as he spoke.

"I was drawn to her right away, but avoided saying anything. I was pretty sure she was just as taken with me, but other than a shy smile now and then, she never let on. There was the language barrier, too. Then one night, after I'd been there about two months, she slipped into my hut and that was that. I was never sure her father approved, but he never said anything. I've never felt so close to someone as I did her. And then, it was just as quickly over."

"What happened?"

"The NVA attacked our village and she was killed."

"The drawing on the bookcase and the other sketches, they're of her, right?"

"Yes."

"And you're sure she died?"

"Yes. No one could have survived that onslaught," Bill said.

"You did."

Bill sat quietly, shaking his head.

Angela

Angela was on the trail for two hours before she realized she'd forgotten to call in since leaving her campsite in Enchanted Valley. The Ranger-in-charge, Frank Burrows, was a stickler for following procedure and he was especially strict with the summer volunteers. She stopped by a fallen cedar tree, whose exposed root system resembled a giant octopus. The typical reception on the wireless radio was poor, at best, but this morning she got right through.

"You're late!" Frank Burrows said.
"I know. Just got distracted."
"Where are you?"
"A mile or so from the chalet, starting the climb to the Pass."
"Everything okay?"
"Yes, fine. I've only seen one hiking party this morning and there were only two campsites at the chalet that were used last night."

"All right, Angela. This is your second summer as a volunteer Ranger, so you should know how important it is to keep in contract. Call me when you get to Anderson Pass Camp, or before if you spot something that needs attention. Carl Wilson is at Anderson, by the way, and he could use your help putting a new hand rail on a log bridge."

"Okay, Mr. Burrows. Sorry about being late."

Angela Rhodes would be a junior at Oregon's Lynnfield College in the fall and wanted to work in the Park the next summer, too. Having the senior Park Ranger mad at her was not a step in the right direction. It had been hard to find a summer job in 1978, but after seeing the poster in the dorm about the volunteer program, she'd applied and was amazed when she got the interview.

She was even more amazed when she was hired. Now, in her second summer in the Olympics, she wanted nothing more than to come back again next summer before she graduated. She loved the outdoors and her job. Angela was seriously contemplating changing her major from education to forestry and applying for a job as a Park Ranger.

Another hour passed and she decided to stop for some lunch. She knew of a spot along the river that was just a few yards down a bank from the main trail. Some hemlock trees that would provide welcome shade from the noonday sun encircled the clearing. Even at 3000-foot elevation it was well into the seventies by eleven and although she rarely burned, Angela sensed that her legs and arms had had enough exposure for one day.

She dropped her pack and took off her baseball cap, letting her long dark blond hair fall to her shoulders. She found the peanut butter sandwich she'd made that morning and sat on a log at the river's edge.

It was then that she sensed movement in a clump of scrub trees and tall ferns that lined the trail above her.

Angela had seen deer at this spot before. Maybe she'd disturbed one. They loved the tender new grasses and cattails along the river's edge. She looked again. No movement, and only the sound of the river water lapping against the rocks.

She finished her sandwich, put the wrapper in her pack and took a drink from her canteen. *Time to move on.* She pulled her sun-streaked hair back into a ponytail. *There it was again! A patch* of *color? Blue or black, though, not light brown like a deer. A bear?* She'd met a black bear on the trail last year and remembered her fright.

Donning her pack, Angela looked again in the direction of the trail. Nothing. *Probably just the wind. But the glimpse of color? Got to get going. Come on, Angela, get a grip!*

As she climbed the steep and rocky trail to the Pass, Angela more than once glanced behind her, but by the time she got to the Anderson Glacier Trail, she decided it had all been in her imagination. *Spooky, though.*

The rest of the day, she helped Carl Wilson finish debarking the branch from a fir tree and fitting it to the forked uprights he'd already nailed to the edge of the log bridge. For jobs like this one, the Rangers usually relied on a volunteer trail crew, but the one assigned to their section was repairing the trail to Flapjack Lakes.

"There, that should do it," Carl said, pounding in the last nail using the back of his hand ax. "I'm glad to get rid of the extra weight. These nails are more like spikes, but they'll hold for a while. Thanks Angela."

"Are you staying here tonight, or going back to Honeymoon Meadows?"

"Staying here."

Anderson Pass Shelter, often called "Camp Siberia," was primarily an emergency-use-only shelter, but in mid-summer, hikers often stayed the night. Unfortunately, at the campsite's elevation no fires were allowed, plus there was no pit toilet and few level spots to pitch a tent.

"Good. I'd like some company tonight," said Angela.

"What's wrong? You're usually alone on the trail most of the time. Don't believe all the crap about a Sasquatch or huge, hairy mountain man do you?" He laughed. "Even tried blaming him for that missing mule last year. Then they found the dumb animal wandering around in the valley."

"No! Nothing in particular, I guess." She hesitated. "I did get a bit spooked on the trail today, though. I just would feel better if you were here tonight."

RW realized he'd followed the girl too far this time and would not be able to get back to the cave before dark. Twice before he'd watched her, but today, he'd been careless and thought sure she'd spotted him crouching in the tall ferns. Bill warned him about strangers, but there was something about this girl that captivated him. His usual caution had given way to an overwhelming sense of curiosity.

Last month he'd been gone overnight when he took the wrong trail coming back from the Duckabush and Bill was plenty upset. He was going to be unhappy again. RW told Bill about the first time he'd seen the girl in the ranger uniform and he'd been told, well not exactly told, instructed in strong language would be more accurate, to stay away from her.

Better find a place to bed down for the night, he thought.

RW headed for a familiar site a mile down the trail where several downed cedars lay across each other. There wasn't much cover if it rained, but it should be fine for the night and as it was several yards off the path, he would be hidden.

By the time he got there the light was fading fast, so he unrolled the blanket he always carried and crawled under the protection of dead trees. *Maybe he wouldn't tell Bill about the girl.*

But he did, and Bill was surprisingly unconcerned.

"There's bound to be more hikers as summer goes on. Just don't get seen, especially by the girl. She's a Ranger and would definitely be suspicious of you the way you're dressed."

RW saw her again one more time the summer of 1979, but stayed a good distance away so there was no chance she would catch sight of him.

Hal Burton

Descent from Anderson Pass into Enchanted Valley

Life in a Cave

He glanced up from his reading. "I think I was a Boy Scout."

"Oh really, how'd you reach that conclusion?"

RW was looking at the newspapers they'd brought back from Amanda Park the day before.

"These uniforms look familiar. See here." He handed Bill the Sunday magazine section from Aberdeen's *The Daily World*. "I recognize the pictures of Camp Parsons, too."

The magazine was open to a feature story on the Boy Scout Camp, near Brinnon on Hood Canal. The title of the article was, "Camp Parsons Marks Start of 61st Year."

RW continued. "Look, it says Parsons is one of the oldest Scout camps in the US. They held their first session in 1919."

"Yes I see," said Bill. "So what makes you think you've been there before?"

"I don't know for sure, but something clicked when I looked at those pictures. Especially the ones of the beach area."

"You know, I went to Camp Parsons when I was in Scouts," said Bill.

"You did. When?"

"A long time ago." Bill handed the magazine back to RW. Then, changing the subject as he often did when it involved his past, "Did you see the article about Mount St. Helens? They think all the recent earthquakes mean it might blow soon."

"Yeah, wouldn't that be something. Has it ever erupted before?"

"Not for hundreds of years as far as I know," said Bill.

Their second winter together hadn't been as easy as the first, (record cold, as he was to learn), and as much as they'd prepared, by mid-April most of their food stores were in short supply. Bill was glad when the snow started melting and they could hike into Amanda Park. It had taken most of two days.

It had been RW's first time and he was upset when Bill told him to stay out of sight while he bought supplies. He argued and finally Bill relented. RW remembered their conversation.

"You wait over there by the Chevron station. Try to stay around the side, away from the gas pumps."

"Come on, I hiked a long way over a muddy trail to get here. This is my first time. At least can I go to the library?"

"Okay, you go over there." He pointed across the highway. "Leave your pack with me and meet me back here at two."

"I don't have a watch, remember."

"The library will," Bill had said as he turned to enter the Mercantile. "Keep in mind, you don't have a card, so don't try to check out any books. If there's something you want I'll get it for you."

He had been a few minutes late, but Bill seemed not to notice and he helped him load the packs. Other than Edie Cox, the storeowner, no one paid them much attention. Even the librarian had seemed uninterested when RW returned with Bill.

Voices from the Mountain

RW got a book on volcanoes, one on early explorations on the Olympic Peninsula and the new Ludlum novel. Bill checked out "The Source" by James Michener.

The extra weight in their packs had made the hike back to Graves Creek a challenge.

"Remember, we have to return these books in a month, so one of us will have to hike back."

"Maybe I'll go by myself," RW said.

"Maybe you will."

It rained steadily, as it only can on the "wet side" of the Olympics and both men spent the days reading their new books and more of the newspapers Bill had gotten at the store.

"Any more memories coming back?"

"No. Well, maybe. When I was reading about the fire they had at the Christmas tree farm near Forks, I had a recollection of hiding behind some Christmas trees and then riding with somebody in a truck filled with trees."

"That's not odd. Probably proves you're a Christian rather than a Hindu. Or maybe you just worked in a tree lot at Christmas time," he chuckled.

"Come on, be serious. Why would I be hiding?"

"Don't know." Then more sincerely, "Do you remember the name of the other person in the truck?"

"Maybe. Something like Floyd or Boyd," RW answered.

"What kind of truck?"

Without hesitation RW replied. "A Chevy."

"You should be writing all these memories in your log."

"I am. It's getting pretty full."

Bill sensed, but hadn't broached the subject yet, that RW was ready to return to "society." It was hard to believe that it was almost two years since he'd found him. More and more, Bill was tempted to reveal some of his strong suspicions.

However, RW's remembrances of his distant past and identity were still hidden away, even though more frequently he would say that this or that was familiar. The day before when they watched some early-season campers with a canoe, he told Bill that he remembered rowing in a boat like a canoe, only longer and with several oars on each side.

"You were probably on a rowing crew."

"Crew. That does sound familiar and someone yelling at me, 'stroke, stroke'."

"That proves it, I had a friend in Nam that rowed crew in college and he used to tell me all about his races. You must have rowed on a college crew, but where," said Bill?

RW hesitated, then, "I don't know, maybe Washington?"

Lately they'd had many a similar conversation and quite frequently, Bill revealed more of his past to RW.

"Did you go to college, Bill?"

"Yes, as a matter of fact, at the University of Washington. Graduated, too."

RW set down the book on volcanoes and stood, stretching his legs and arms. He walked to the entrance and pulled back the tarp.

"Looks like it stopped raining and I need some exercise, so I'll go check the snares. Want to come along?"

"No, you go ahead. Remember, it still gets dark early."

"Yes, I know. You're starting to act like my big brother protector, again. I'll be back early."

The trail in the Enchanted Valley wasn't as mucky and slippery as the one on the descent from the cave, but it still made for sloppy walking and his once clean boots were now heavily mud-caked. The sun made an appearance, though, and that brightened his spirits.

RW noticed a set of footprints heading opposite of the direction he was going and guessed they had been made that morning. The heavy rains from the previous day would have wiped out traces of older imprints. *Probably heading for the campground near the chalet.* He walked on. *What a great day.*

A distant scream broke his reverie. He couldn't tell for sure from where it had come, as the surrounding cliffs provided perfect walls for echoes. *There it was again!* Definitely back the way he had come from and sounding like a female voice. RW broke into a run, almost falling as his boot slipped on a hat lying in the middle of the path. He stopped and picked it up. The distinctive badge of a Park Ranger glistened in the morning sunlight.

Breaking out of the protective cluster of alders, RW had an unimpeded view of the chalet and the meadows surrounding it. He also had clear sight of a bear that was furiously pawing at the door. As he ducked behind the nearby outhouse, he once again heard a scream, now more loudly and definitely coming from the chalet.

He'd been in the old chalet and guessed the door wouldn't hold up to much force before it would fall in. Bill told him that the Enchanted Valley Chalet was built in 1930 as a hotel, a short-lived enterprise. Now, the three-story building was used as a shelter and maintained by the Park Service.

As he watched, the bear seemed to lose interest and walked around to the back, out of RW's sight. He was about to come out of hiding when the bear, with two cubs following along behind, came around the other side. They were heading his way. *Now what to do?*

He crouched down and was as still as he could be. If the mother bear didn't get his scent he should be safe. It was frustrating, though, not to be able to see what was happening. Finally, after what seemed like forever and not seeing the bear pass on his right, he rose slightly and peeked around the outhouse. At first he didn't see her, but then he spotted the mother and her charges going down the trail to the south and away from the chalet. He was glad he didn't have to use his bow and arrow. He waited a couple more minutes before emerging and then cautiously headed to the chalet, still with an arrow ready in his *Grizzly* bow just in case the mother returned.

"Hello. The bear's gone." No answer. He approached the claw-marked door and again called out. "Hello, are you all right?" Still no response. Then faintly, "Yes, I'm okay. Are you sure he's gone?"

"It was a she, but yes, she's gone."

"All right."

The door opened slowly, but just part way. RW recognized the uniformed girl he'd seen on the trail last summer. She looked at him curiously, her expression apprehensive, then softening.

"Thanks, and by the way, I knew it was female."

She opened the door the rest of the way and stepped out, extending her hand. "I'm Angela, Angela Rhodes, and you?"

Rather than answer, RW shrugged his shoulders and turned.

"Wait. I want to know who helped save me."

RW hesitated. "I didn't save you, just hid till the bear went away. Anyway, you were lucky you got inside. A mother with her cubs is a dangerous thing."

"I know and I was stupid. I was curious when I heard some racket and saw some swishing in the bushes by the riverbank. As I got near, two bear cubs came romping out."

"Then what happened," said RW, caught up in her story and captivated by her sparkling blue eyes.

"That's when I saw the mother on the other side of the river. Unfortunately, she saw me at the same time."

"And you ran?"

"Yes! I fell once in the trail and almost didn't make it back to the chalet."

"Oh, I almost forgot," RW said, and walked back to the outhouse. When he returned he was holding Angela's ranger hat. "Here, this must be yours."

It was the brightest smile he'd ever seen. "Thanks a second time," she said. "Now, are you going to tell me your name?"

"RW. I'm, ah, called RW."

Angela couldn't tell how old he was, but guessed he wasn't much older than she. His shoulder length dark hair and full beard covered most of his features. He was tall, she figured over six feet, as she was five-six and RW was easily one head taller. He certainly didn't look like the typical backpacker. For sure his clothes didn't come from REI or Eddie Bauer. The only thing that appeared store-bought was the bow that hung from a leather strap on his shoulder. It looked like it was made from black fiberglass, tightly strung and no toy.

"And where do you come from, RW? You look like you've been camping out here for quite a while."

He was abruptly aware of what he must look like in his threadbare clothing and his unkempt hair. He felt he should go before she probed too much. Yet he was strongly drawn to her just as he had been from afar the previous summer.

"I've got to go. I'm, ah, from Amanda Park and I've got to get back."

"Amanda Park? I don't remember seeing you before; I'm in there for supplies all the time. Wait!"

But he was walking away, not turning back this time.

"Can't we talk some more?" Angela wanted to know about this strange man. She didn't buy his story about Amanda Park. Still, he was a complete stranger. Maybe she should let it go.

RW continued a short distance and turned. *She's beautiful*, he thought. The sun shown on Angela's tanned face, making the natural color of her full lips appear even redder.

He's staring at me, she realized.

"Talk ...ah ... I." Then, without wavering, "Sure, why not," he said.

Angela smiled. "In case you haven't figured it out, I'm a summer Park Ranger volunteer and I use the chalet as home base. We could meet here or in Amanda Park sometime," she said.

"I figured it out. How about here at the chalet."

"Wouldn't it be easier in town where you live?"

He hesitated, now on the proverbial horns of a dilemma. "I'm out here a lot. The chalet will be fine."

"How about next Wednesday, then. About this time?"

"Okay. What time is it. I forgot my watch."

"Just after ten. So, I'll see you. " She started to walk away, then turned back. "By the way, you know, hunting's not allowed in the park."

"I know." And with that he started down the trail, thinking, *Now I've done it! Bill is really going to be mad!*

Enchanted Valley

Bill couldn't believe it.

"You actually talked to her?" he said, trying not to sound too incredulous.

RW nodded. Bill didn't sound half as upset as RW thought he might be. He shifted his weight on the stool.

"She thinks you're from Amanda Park?" Bill grinned.

"Yes." RW turned, avoiding Bill's eyes.

"Look at me! I guess that's about as good an answer as any. Of course you could have said you lived in a cave with an old Viet Nam vet," he said, his grin widening.

"I know, and I did hesitate lying about Amanda Park."

"Don't worry about it," Bill said. "However, you're going to have to face the truth eventually. She'll probably ask around, especially if she's as interested in you as you are in her."

"What do you mean?" he atypically blushed.

Bill chuckled. "You know damn well what I mean. I think you'd better consider what, if anything, you'd tell this Angela about me the next time you meet. I gather from what you say that you do plan to meet her again?" Bill rose, softly patted RW on the shoulder and walked out of the cave.

RW stood and followed his mentor. "Yes, I do." Bill was right. He'd better get his act together before Wednesday.

He crossed the river several hundred yards northwest of the chalet. For the present, RW didn't want Angela to see from which direction he came. He guessed he was plenty early and sat down on a log at the river's edge, near one of the campsites. He looked at his reflection in a pool of calm water. He had to admit, he looked a lot better with the haircut and beard trim Bill had given him. Even the kidding was worth it.

Smoke rose from the chalet's chimney. *She must be there already*, he thought, then remembered the chalet was her home base and that she'd probably been there the night before. *Might as well go.*

She was sitting on the top porch step drinking from a blue and gray mug emblazoned with a ferocious looking cat.

"Good morning, you're early." She raised the mug to him.

"Nice mug. Weird looking cat, though," RW said.

"He's not a cat, he's a Lynx, Lynnfield's mascot."

"Oh, sorry," suppressing a snicker. "Coffee smells good."

"It is good. My boss at the Quinault Station gets it at Swanson's in Aberdeen. Want some?"

"Sure." RW followed her into the chalet.

"That was really something on Saturday, wasn't it," she said, without turning around.

Uncertain what she meant, he mumbled assent.

"You did hear about the eruption didn't you? It was all over the news. We even felt the quake in Amanda Park. Didn't you?"

"Oh sure. Ah, yes, that was something."

She poured him some coffee in a plain brown cup. "Here. You're really not a very good liar, you know. You don't live in Amanda Park, do you?"

"No."

"Mount St. Helens erupted on Saturday. How could you not know about that?"

He was had and he knew it.

"Maybe you'd like to tell me the truth and you're probably not too surprised to hear that no one in Amanda Park has any idea who you are."

"Well, the irony is, I don't either." He laughed quietly. "I'm just like Jason Bourne, no identity."

"Why don't you start by telling me your real name? I'm sure Robert Ludlum could come up with a better moniker than RW."

"All right, but it's a long story with lots of answers I don't have."

"That's fine, I've got lots of time. I may even have some answers for you. By the way, it's nice to see your face."

She was fascinated by his story and she had to admit, equally fascinated with him.

"Wow. You don't remember anything before Bill found you?"

"Little bits and pieces keep popping into my head, but no, not much since about two years ago," RW said.

"Has Bill ever tried to find out what happened to you? It's odd that he wouldn't have at least asked around or read something in the newspaper."

"No, I don't think so or he would have told me. You have to remember that he only makes a couple trips a year and other than a library card, which is not even in his real name, he avoids any contact. It's really only since I came along that he even ventures out much at all."

"How does he get food and supplies?"

"What we don't catch or forage, he buys at the store in Amanda Park."

"Where does he get the money?"

"You'd have to ask him that."

Angela wondered whether it was time to tell RW what she had learned and had pieced together about his possible identity, but he answered that question for her.

"You said you might have some answers."

"Yes. Maybe, but I'm a little hesitant."

"Why? I've told you everything I know, even some vague recollections I haven't told Bill."

Angela poured herself some more coffee and walked past him. "Okay. Come on let's go out on the porch, it's too nice a morning to stay in here."

RW tagged along and although he tried to avoid gawking, his eyes unavoidably followed her. He speculated that a trim and womanly shape was hidden beneath the ill-fitting Park Service uniform. She sat down and patted the spot next to her.

"Sit here beside me." She took a drink, then a deep breath and set her cup down as much as to say, *So here goes.*

"When I was convinced you were lying to me about living in Amanda Park, I started reading the back issues of the local newspapers because I remembered my boss telling me about a missing hiker back in 1978. The hiker would have been about your age. The papers only went back to last year, so yesterday I used the library's microfiche machine."

"A missing hiker," RW said, remembering Bill's speculation about what had happened. "Bill always told me that I'd probably lost my footing and tumbled down the moraine. That doesn't mean it was me, though."

"Maybe not. The microfiche article said the missing hiker was with three friends and when they woke up the second morning, he was gone."

"Gone! But how... I don't see, ah," RW was suddenly quiet. He nodded his head almost as if he was remembering something.

"The hiker's friends names were Pete, Gordy and Larry. Does that ring any bells?"

"No, not really."

"How about the name Ray?"

"No. Was he another friend?"

"That's the name of the missing hiker. Ray, Ray Wellsford."

"Ray Wellsford," he said, slowly sounding it out.

She smiled. "Notice that the names start with R and W?"

RW looked at his boots. "That could just be coincidence."

"I think it's more than that," she said. "You sure don't seem very excited, Ray." She stood up. "I'd be jumping up and down about now."

"I just can't believe the information was there all the time. Was there a picture with the articles?"

"No. I think the library in Aberdeen would have more extensive files, but I haven't gone there."

"So you're convinced I'm the lost hiker, Ray Wellsford?"

"It sure makes sense."

RW rose and without saying anything, walked down the trail to the river. Angela put her coffee cup down and followed him to the river's edge.

"The Quinault is high this time of year."

Angela stopped next to him and reached for his hand. "Yes, it is."

"What now?" he asked, giving her hand a squeeze.

"I made a copy of the articles for you and I guess it's up to you what you do next. I would think there's a family out there that would want to know you're alive and of course, I'd want to know what happened to me on that hike."

"If I'm Ray," he said.

"Yes, that's true." She released his hand, smiled and reaching up, tenderly pushed the hair from his eyes. "I'll be glad to help and I'm sure your friend Bill will, too."

"Maybe you'd like to meet him? Do you want to come with me?"

"Oh, I don't know. Won't he be mad if I suddenly appear? Besides, I promised to check on a rockslide near White Creek."

"If it's all right, I'll go with you and then we can see Bill tomorrow, only you've got to promise to never tell anyone where we live or about Bill. Okay?"

The rockslide had destroyed the log bridge that once spanned the creek and crossing now entailed climbing down one pile of rocks and up another. Angela told RW she was glad he came along, as she never could have considered replacing the bridge without his help. It became a moot point however, as there were only short sections of the original log scattered around and lacking heavier tools, there was no way they would be able to fell a new tree to take its place.

All they could do was rearrange the rocks to make the creek passing less tricky. Angela marked the path with several orange colored strips of cloth she brought.

"That about does it. It's starting to get dark," Angela said. "Thanks for the help." She offered him her canteen.

"You're welcome. Glad I could help."

"Time to head back. The offer still stands to spend the night in the chalet, if, as you say, Bill won't be concerned."

"Okay, you win, given the choice of sleeping outside or inside where it's nice and warm. Bill's used to my absences."

"Let's go then," she said and took the lead for the three-mile hike back to the Enchanted Valley and the chalet. Neither of them said much as they walked, but each silently contemplated the night ahead with its potential complications.

Darkness took over quicker than they'd anticipated, and RW had to walk almost on top of Angela in order to see the narrow path in the beam of her flashlight. Not that he minded being close to her.

"I should have brought my flashlight." *That's odd,* he thought. *What's that expression, deja vu?*

"That's okay, we're just about there."

She was right and once they left the dense covering of trees, it lightened up and the chalet came into view.

"It's going to be a nice night, how about we roast hotdogs outside over the fire pit? No bugs to bother us this time of year," Angela said.

―――

The fireside conversation had been, at best, sporadic. It reminded Angela of the scene from Casablanca where the Bogart and Bergman characters sit at the table in the lounge and don't say anything, even though they both want to. Feeling a similar awkwardness, Angela thought of saying, "play it again Sam", to ease the tension. She nuzzled into his shoulder.

"I'll take one of the beds in the loft. You can have your choice of the bunks on the first floor."

"Fine," RW said, posed like the famous Rodin statue.

"What are you thinking so deeply about?" Angela asked.

"Remember, when we were walking and I commented about not bringing my flashlight?"

"Yes, but you're still not worried about that, are you?"

"No. It's just ..." He stopped and then continued. "I had a vivid memory of another time when I was hiking and chastised myself for forgetting a flashlight. Then I remembered falling."

"You mean falling down, like tripping?"

"No. Really falling. Like sailing through the air."

He was silent again. Angela poked a stick in the fire and spread out the coals. Then reaching across, took his hand.

"It might not mean anything or it may be another piece of the puzzle. Right now, I think it's time to turn in. It's been a long day."

"You're right. Another puzzle piece, maybe." He rose, and offering her his hand, gently pulled her up from the canvas chair. "Thanks for the meal. Sorry I wasn't more talkative."

"That's alright, I really enjoyed your company. It gets lonely out here."

They both blushed at this moment, but in the dark, neither could see. RW held Angela's hand as they walked to the door. Releasing her hand, he put both arms around her.

"Thanks again for a great night. I'm going to wash up."

"Yes, it was." She stood on her tiptoes and kissed RW on the cheek. "Goodnight."

Wood Carvings and Revelations

Angela rose before six only to find RW awake and busily adding wood to the still hot coals in the old Franklin stove. The previous night's awkwardness lingered and after a soft "good morning", Angela put fresh coffee grounds in the pot and headed to the lone bathroom in the chalet. When she returned, RW had the fire roaring, had set out the box of cornflakes and was mixing two glasses of Tang. She decided to break the ice.

"Good to see we're both morning people."

He laughed. "Yes, I guess it is."

After finishing breakfast, Angela tried to reach her boss, Frank Burrows at the Quinault Station. RW cleared the table and poured them each some more coffee while Angela called again, but as before, got only static on the two-way radio. When the third attempt failed she commented that maybe the ash cloud from the St. Helens' eruption was causing interference. Now, ten minutes later, Angela had put trail mix and a few personal items in her backpack, filled two canteens and was lacing up her boots when RW returned from the bathroom.

"All set to go?"

"Almost. Give me a few more minutes to try again to get Frank on the radio. I need to let him know in what general area I'll be hiking."

Over the sound of the radio static they both heard the three loud knocks on the door of the chalet.

"Maybe Frank decided to come here today," said RW.

"Frank wouldn't knock, he'd just holler and come in."

The sunlight made it difficult to see, but RW had little doubt who it was. For sure it wasn't Frank Burrows. Angela had a good guess and she was right.

"Angela, this is my good friend, Bill O'Hara."

He wasn't as old as Angela had imagined from RW's description, and she thought he looked more like one of N. C. Wyeth's illustrations of Robinson Crusoe than the mythical mountain man he was surmised to be.

Similar to Wyeth's depictions of Crusoe, he wore a fur hat and coat, had an old wicker pack, and a hand axe protruded from his belt. Instead of the parasol and rifle that Crusoe was often pictured with, Bill carried his *Grizzly* bow, and a full arrow sheath was slung near his pack.

"Come in Bill," Angela offered, even though without any hesitation he had already stepped over the transom.

"Thought I'd better see what you were up to," he said, looking at RW.

"Please, take off your pack and coat and have a seat," Angela said. "The coffee's probably still hot and I can get the stove going again."

"Thanks, I will, and coffee sounds great."

RW was at a loss for words. Bill seldom ventured out and now he was sitting with him and Angela. Thinking about it, he was glad that they hadn't surprised Bill by going to the cave and in retrospect; it had probably been a bad idea. Now, nervous in front of his companion of almost two years, he blurted out the first thing that came into his mind.

"Angela found some information at the library about a missing hiker and we think that maybe it was me. I mean that he was I, oh damn, that I'm the missing hiker."

"Is that right," Bill said, accepting the offered cup from Angela and taking off his pack. "When was that?"

"In June of 1978," Angela answered.

"Well, that would be just about right," Bill said. "What was the hiker's name?"

"Ray Wellsford," RW answered, pronouncing the name slowly, as if trying to recognize it.

Bill sipped his coffee, but said nothing. He carefully laid his bow and arrows on the floor next to his pack.

"What an unusual pack," Angela said, breaking the silence.

"Yes, it is. I converted it from an old fishing creel and use it when I go into town."

"It's what he uses to carry his carvings," said RW.

"Carvings?" Angela said, wishing she hadn't changed the subject, but curious nevertheless.

"Here, I'll show you," Bill said, reaching into the pack and pulling out a carved figurine of an eagle, about six inches high.

She was momentarily flabbergasted and uncharacteristically at a loss for words. Then it came to her.

"I've seen one much like this before, but can't remember where."

"Probably at the Mercantile in Amanda Park. They buy just about all I can do. Keeps me looking for good pieces of alder."

"Yes. That's it! Now I remember, and they sell others, too, like bears and mountain goats. Edie at the store has them right on the shelf next to the magazine rack."

Bill reached back into the pack. "You mean like these," he said handing Angela two figures of a bear with a cub.

"Yes." She turned the bear carvings over in her hand. "You're very good, you know."

"Helps pass the time. RW writes, I carve." He turned to look at RW who'd been silent during the interchange. "Maybe I should start calling you Ray."

"Then you think it's true, Bill?"

"Could be. Let's see what you've got," Bill said to Angela.

Angela retrieved the copies of the newspaper articles and handed them to Bill.

He briefly looked through them and turned to RW.

"Actually, I've seen these before. You see I've known almost from the beginning that you may be Ray Wellsford."

"You never told me!" RW said in disbelief.

"Listen, I'm sorry about that, but I would have when I thought you were ready."

Bill told them about his first trips to Amanda Park when RW had been well enough to leave alone. How he, much like Angela, had used the library's records. How he had been tempted to call the authorities and Ray's parents but didn't for fear that he himself would be discovered. Then finally his decision to wait until RW was healed both mentally and physically.

"You have to understand, that two years ago I was a mental case myself and was avoiding any kind of contact. I just couldn't take a chance," Bill said.

"But how about last year or last month! I just don't get it!" RW stared in disbelief at his friend of two years.

"I know. Time just passed by and you still didn't seem ready. Believe me, I thought I was doing the right thing."

"Did you ever find a picture of the missing hiker?" Angela asked.

"No, only a description, but it sure fits RW to a tee."

RW shook his head. "I still don't get it. You even knew I had parents that might be alive and you never told me."

"I was going to, I swear. In fact, I had planned to take you again to the spot where I found you to see if maybe it would jog a few more memories."

"Why didn't you?"

"You met Angela and I didn't know how to handle the situation. I figured she might do some investigating and decided to wait and see."

RW sat quietly for several minutes. Then he rose and walked over to Bill, offering his hand.

"Sorry I got so pissed. I owe you my life and I can understand why you waited."

Their conversation was interrupted by a voice on the wireless radio. "Angela, Angela, this is Frank, come in please."

Angela pressed the receiver key and answered. "Frank, yes, this is Angela. I've been trying to get you all morning."

"I'm glad you're still there, we have a serious problem in the Upper O'Neil Creek area. A father and son are missing. Jim Krones just called it in. I'd like you to get there and help in the search."

Angela got some additional details about the missing campers and turned her attention back to Bill and RW.

"Looks like that's it for me today. Bill, I'm glad we met and RW, I mean Ray, I think you've got a lot to think about."

"Ray and I can help with the search, if it's alright," said Bill, "I was going into Amanda Park today anyway."

"Sure, we'd welcome the help," Angela answered. Then looking at Bill, "Are you sure you want the extra exposure?"

"I'm beginning to think I'm not going to have much choice. I just ask that you don't tell anyone about the cave for now. That's something I'll have to think about."

"Okay, let's go," Angela said.

"When we get back Ray, let's take that hike up to Anderson Pass and see if we can't jog some more memories," Bill said.

It had been a steady uphill grind since they crossed over White Creek and passed the junction with the trail to O'Neil Pass.

As Bill and Ray hiked they chatted about how the missing father and son had shown up at their group's campsite two hours late, safe and unhurt. Then, how ironical and comical (at least to them) it had been when one of the search party ended up lost and they spent the rest of the day searching for him. He had been found three hours later, embarrassed, but unscathed. Bill and Ray had said their goodbyes and hiked to Amanda Park.

Now, two days later, they were nearing Anderson Pass Camp and the spot where Bill had found Ray almost two years before. Even though it was early June, at 3600-foot elevation the temperature hovered near freezing and the recently fallen snow was only a few feet off the trail's edge.

"Well, here we are," said Bill, taking off his pack at the campsite's perimeter.

"A bit more snow than our last trip," Ray said, removing his pack and setting it by Bill's.

"Why don't we go over to the rim above where I found you?"

Ray followed Bill to the edge and looked down.

"Anything?" asked Bill.

"Not really. Just like last time, only a dull sense that I stood here before, but that really doesn't prove anything."

Suddenly the snow-saturated ground gave way and Ray started losing his footing, falling forward. Bill, who was standing a few paces behind grabbed him and pulled him back.

"That was close!" Bill said.

Ray nodded, but said nothing. He just stared off towards Anderson Glacier, almost as in a trance.

"I remember!" Ray said.

"You mean about being here before?"

"Yes, but also what happened to me. Somebody hit me from behind!"

"One of your friends?"

"It had to be one of them. Who else?"

The plan developed slowly over the next several days. After first contacting his parents, stage one would be to contact both the local authorities and the Seattle Police. Likely that would result in the story being published in the newspapers.

The second stage would be to contact each of his friends from the hike and arrange a one-on-one meeting. Ray argued over how soon and how much to involve the police in this phase, but Bill had won out.

Bill also had a suggestion for the second stage "contact" phase that would add some drama to process.

"It will take me some time, but if I start now, I should be done in a couple of days."

"Do you have enough alder?"

"No, but we can get some tomorrow when we check the traps."

"For now, you need to work on the letter that will go with our little surprise."

"What if one or more of them doesn't respond? You know, we don't even know for sure that they're around."

Bill rose and patted Ray on the shoulder. "That's why you need to contact your folks right away, for their help."

Brother Pete

Because Pete always read the sports section of the *Seattle Times* before anything else, Betty spotted the story first.

"There's an article in the paper about Ray Wellsford being found!" Betty said, looking over the newspaper at her husband.

"What! You're kidding. Let me see."

"It's here, right on the first page."

Pete Fairchild took the Sunday morning edition of the *Seattle Times* from his wife and read the front-page article.

"My God, after over two years and all the searching and he suddenly turns up." His hand shook as he laid the paper on the table in their apartment kitchen. "Everyone thought he was dead."

"They never found his body, did they?"

"No."

"You should try and get in touch with him, Pete. He was your best friend."

"The article doesn't say anything about where he is now, just that he contacted his folks."
"Do they still live on Queen Anne Hill?"
"I don't know. Probably. I haven't talked to his dad or mom in over a year," Pete said.
"Well, that's what I'd do, call them."
"I still can't believe it. I wonder if Larry and Gordy know?"
"Maybe you should call them, too."

Pete Fairchild didn't graduate with his class from the University of Washington. He dropped out of school during the first quarter of his junior year. His dad thought that the trauma of Ray's disappearance had a lot to do with it. His girlfriend Betty Fowler thought it had just as much to do with all the turmoil in the fraternity House over the unsolved rape. Poor grades were a big contributor, but his dad's assessment was the closest to the truth.

After his wife died, Pete's dad, Orville, pored himself into his work at University Pontiac and rose to the position of general manager by the time Pete started college.

It was in the service department at University Pontiac where Pete starting working when he quit school. He hated his job and kept telling himself that it was temporary.

Although Betty Fowler dated other boys during her junior and senior years, Pete still considered her his girlfriend. She was the perfect woman as far as he was concerned. As he often told himself, his love was big enough for both of them.

Undaunted by his self-perceived lower status, Pete continued to pursue Betty, often spending his whole paycheck on dinner or an expensive present.

Hal Burton

Two months before Betty's graduation, Pete proposed. They married and moved into the Wallingford Apartments after a weeklong honeymoon in Victoria, British Columbia.

When Pete, Larry and Gordy couldn't find Ray that fateful summer, they first assumed he was off having a morning constitutional, but a half hour later they got concerned when he didn't answer their calls. They started searching the area after agreeing to meet back at the campsite in half an hour. Pete later recalled it was Gordy who checked the area near the drop-off, but no one had answered when he called out Ray's name. He remembered that Larry had crawled most of the way down the bank, but still had not seen anything.

Because his leg was still tender, Larry and Pete had decided that Gordy should stay at the campsite to rest while they hiked back to try and find help. They went to Honeymoon Meadows and then Diamond Meadows, but no one was there. Though it was getting dark, they had continued on to Big Timber where they found Ranger Sullivan and he alerted the stations at Dosewallips, Kalaloch, and Park headquarters in Port Angeles.

A search party of three Rangers had left from Dose Forks at dawn and after joining with Pete, Larry, and Ranger Bob Sullivan at Big Timber, they hiked steadily for six miles, reaching Anderson Pass Camp at two. Pete remembered that it had started snowing the last mile of their hike and continued as they spread out to search the surrounding area. At nightfall they gave up for the day and ended up pitching their tents on the new snow. The Coast Guard helicopter from Neah Bay arrived over the area in the morning, but low clouds hampered their search. On the ground, a light snow continued to fall.

The newspaper stories that appeared over the next week told how the search team had scoured the area. Ranger Jerry Helspath from Kalaloch and the trail crew working near O'Neil Creek had been pressed into service. The only lost thing they found, however, was their missing pack mule, wandering aimlessly along the Enchanted Valley Trail.

Pete got the letter with the small package in the mail the day after he called Gordy.

Brother Gordy

The *Spokesman Review* didn't carry the story about Ray Wellsford's miraculous reappearance, so Gordy Shandy didn't hear about it until he got a phone call from Pete Fairchild.

Gordy had been home a week and was still unpacking four years of accumulated stuff. His parents attended the graduation ceremonies in Seattle and then had headed back to Spokane leaving Gordy to attend two graduation parties and clear out of the fraternity House. He would return to the University in September to start work toward his Master's Degree in Biology.

After his sophomore year Gordy appeared to lose interest in everything but his studies. Any relationships he had were superficial, even his interaction with Larry and Pete became strained and mechanical-like. In his eyes, attending the graduation party at the fraternity House and the reception at the Dean's house had been a duty rather than a pleasure. He hated that he'd let himself be talked into going.

Gordy had tried to forget about the fateful hike when Ray disappeared. The weeks that followed had been pure hell. Questions, followed by more questions, and then on top of everything, the University police and Seattle cops kept badgering him about the rape at the House. Then when a girl from the Alpha Kappa Sorority was brutally raped the following September, the questioning started all over again.

Ray Wellsford was alive. He hoped that wouldn't open up the rape investigations again.

Pete hadn't been very detailed about Ray's return, only that the new's stories said he had been living in the Olympic Mountains for two years and could be contacted through his parents. *How odd*, thought Gordy. *Surely there was more to the story.*

He had thanked Pete for the call and decided that for the present he would do nothing. *After all*, he thought to himself, *better to let things be. He had grad school to worry about and he could call Ray's folks when he returned to Seattle.*

Gordy's package arrived two days later. Like Pete's it was postmarked Amanda Park, Washington.

Brother Larry

The *Yakima Herald* carried the story about Ray Wellsford's amazing appearance, but Larry didn't see the article until his mom showed it to him. He wondered whether Gordy knew. He'd hitched a ride home with him just a few days before.

Larry's sole focus through his four years at Washington had been on football. He was starting guard his senior year, but disappointed when he'd been picked near the bottom in the fifth round of the draft by the Seattle Seahawks. Still, he planned to show them his stuff at camp in Cheney.

God, he thought, *Ray's alive*. Pete will remind him for sure that he told them they should have looked longer. Hank had reportedly waited at Graves Creek and when they never showed up, driven to the Ranger station at Quinault to report them missing. "What an idiot," Pete had later said. If they had shown up late, he wouldn't have been there. Hank told everyone he was sorry for not staying at Graves Creek.

Not that it had mattered. That's one of the things Larry didn't like about Hank, he was always apologizing for something.

When the package arrived for Larry he opened it immediately. Inside was a small wood carving of four people and a letter addressed to him. He turned the carving over in his hands, holding it up to the light.

Upon close examination he realized it was the carving of four men with packs on their backs. One wore an Australian style hat. *It's Ray and the three of us!*

He set the carving aside and read the letter.

Dear Larry:

I'm sure by now you have heard that I am alive and well. I need to see you.

If you look closely at the enclosed carving you'll notice that only the person with the hat has facial features. That's me, as you've probably guessed. The others have no features. The reason? One of you may be responsible for my disappearance and answerable for the rape at the House that night over two years' ago. But you see, if true, I don't know for sure which one. I draw a blank on that one – hence the blank faces.

I'm going to call you in a few days to suggest where we might meet. I hope you can help be put a "face" on this. You were a good friend.

Ray

Larry set the letter down, his hand trembling. "Crap!" he said aloud. "Just what I need."

His phone rang.

"Hello."

"Larry, this is Gordy."

A few minutes later he got two more calls. One was from Pete.

Council In The Cave

The chattering male squirrel chased the female up and down and around the tall cedar, followed her jump to another tree and repeated the mating ritual that signaled a change of seasons.

"Looks like it will be an early winter," Ray said, watching the madcap race. They'd taken a short break and were now climbing once more.

"Are you sure Bill knows about this?" Angela asked.

"Yes, I told you. He and I met in Amanda Park last week and it was he who suggested we get together at the cave."

"I'm glad you called Quinault, I was going to leave in two days to head back to Lynnfield."

"I thought you were done?"

"No, I have one more semester."

"So you were just going to take off and not say goodbye?"

"Come on, I didn't even know where you were and you did give me your folk's phone number, remember."

Bill's Cave above the Enchanted Valley

"I know. My mom said I should have called earlier," Ray said.

Angela and Ray left Graves Creek Campground after an early breakfast and reached the chalet in the Valley shortly after noon.

"How much farther?"

"Just a few more minutes. You'll see the waterfall when we go around that big rock just ahead," Ray said, pointing at a large outcropping where the trail seemed to end.

"But the trail looks like it stops. Are we climbing over?"

"Be patient."

They'd now been off the main trail for twenty minutes or so and had been following a barely visible path that ran alongside one of the creeks cascading down from Chimney Peak and into the Quinault River. Ray told Angela how Bill had discovered the cave while climbing near a waterfall and how, deciding to leave civilization, had converted his find to a livable dwelling. She was amazed that Bill had lived in the cave for over three years and not been discovered. It was true that few hikers attempted to climb the cliffs above the Valley and those that tried to scale Chimney Peak usually approached from the west side. The waterfall, spectacular as it was, remained unnamed.

As they got closer to the outcropping, Angela could see that the rock actually didn't extend all the way to the bottom intersecting the trail. Rather, from their side, it took on the shape of a man's forehead and nose, with the area under the nose leaving about a four feet gap.

Ray took her hand. "Come on. Duck down and follow me."

The first thing Angela saw when she straightened up on the other side was the waterfall. She'd seen it from the Valley below, but up close she could actually feel the power it possessed, now engorged from the spring rains and snow melt. The second thing she saw, standing just outside the cascading water's mist was a tall, bearded man with a smile on his face.

"Saw you coming up the trail and thought I'd meet you here. "Welcome, Angela. C'mon, you might as well see our humble abode."

That said, Bill disappeared into the mist.

"Just follow me," Ray said to Angela, and taking her hand, led her through the mist onto a shelf behind the falling water and into the cave.

Even though Ray had told her about his cave home, Angela was amazed, first at the shear size and then at how well it was furnished, considering where it was located.

"Pull that tarp closed behind you," Bill said. "As Ray knows, this time of year it gets pretty damp in here."

The first thing Ray noticed were the boxes stacked next to the bookcase and the piles of clothes on the extra bed. Curious, he started to ask, but Bill spoke first.

"So, you sent the letters and the wood figures?"

"Yeah. They should all have them by now," Ray answered.

"I assume you told Angela about your plan?"

"Yes, I did. I am curious, though, why you wanted me to bring her along today."

"Let's hear how your plan is going, first," Bill said.

"It's as much yours as mine," Ray answered and then brought Bill up to date.

He told how he had selected restaurants in Seattle, Yakima and Spokane to meet the letter recipients and would schedule his meetings on three different days. He was going to call them the next day from his folk's home.

When they met, Ray would tell them what had happened to him, would ask each one what he remembered about the hike and especially about the night he was attacked. Finally, he would ask them whom they suspected. Bill quietly listened, and then spoke.

"Three questions. First, what if you don't learn anything that gives you a hint as to who hit you?"

"Then I'm no worse off than before, am I?"

"Maybe not. Okay, second question. What if you think that one of them is the guilty one. What next?"

Angela broke into the conversation. "Yes, what's to protect you if that person thinks you know more than you do. He tried to kill you once, you know."

"That's sort of my third question," Bill said. "When do you involve the police in this?"

"Actually, I already have. It was Detective Sergeant Casper of the Seattle Police that suggested a clever modification to our original plan."

"The same detective Casper that was involved with the rape case, I assume," said Bill.

"Yes." He told Bill and Angela what Casper had suggested.

"You have been busy since you left," Bill said. "It's a risky thing to do, but I can see why he suggested it."

"Look's like you've been busy, too," said Ray, pointing to the boxes.

Bill smiled. "I could tell you had some questions. All right, I guess it's my turn. The boxes probably gave it away. I'm leaving the cave."

He continued, holding up his hand to feign off any interruptions.

"Actually we could have met in Amanda Park or at the Quinault Ranger Station, but I thought this would give Angela a chance to see where you lived and for you to gather up anything you still have here. I also had the ulterior motive of needing some help getting all this stuff out of here."

Neither Ray nor Angela said anything for what seemed like an eternity. Bill rose and walked over to Ray. "Come on, it can't be that much of a shock."

"Where are you going to live?" Ray asked, his tone of voice

and puzzled expression reflecting his disbelief.

"Edie found me a small cabin to rent in Amanda Park."

"Edie at the Mercantile?" Ray asked, still flummoxed.

"Yes, and there's a workshop behind the cabin where I can do my carving and drawings. She thinks that I can make a comfortable living selling my art to her and to the gift shops on the Peninsula."

"Why now. I mean, why all of a sudden?" Angela asked.

"Why not! Frankly, with Ray gone and my need to keep turning out carvings for the store, it just made good sense. The isolation gave me time to sort out my life, but now I need to get back to reality, so to speak."

"What about your mom in Denver?"

"Actually, I've called her from time to time, but there's nothing there for me. I may visit sometime."

"I still can't believe it," said Ray.

"Believe it, Ray, and by the way, there's another cabin near mine for rent. Maybe you and Angela can move in there after this is all over," he said, a broad smile spreading over his face.

"Bill!" Angela shouted.

"Just kidding," but he could tell by the expression (at least on Ray's face), that he'd struck close to home.

"So, that's it, I guess. How about we load up and head for my new digs."

Confrontations

～

Saying goodbye to both Bill and Angela had been hard to do, but Ray knew he would see them both again. He contemplated his relationship with Angela while he waited at the Denny's Restaurant on 15th NW. He knew he had developed strong feelings for her, but wasn't sure how she felt. Ray checked his watch. *Twenty after twelve, Pete's late.*

For a Saturday, the restaurant wasn't very busy, although the traffic on Ballard Avenue had been heavy and Ray had been concerned about being on time. He got up from the bench seat in the lobby and was about to ask the host to be seated, when he spotted Pete coming in the door.

Pete looked much the same as he had two years earlier. *Maybe* a *little older looking*, thought Ray, as he extended his hand to his old friend. "Pete, great to see you. Thanks for coming."

"How could I not, Ray. Your letter and phone call made that pretty clear." He chuckled, though, and Ray saw the person he once called his best friend. *He couldn't be the one… no?*

"Let's get a booth and then we can talk about all of this and you can bring me up to date on your life," Ray said.

As soon as they had ordered, Pete broke the ice and told Ray about his marriage to Betty and his job. Ray listened in silence, just staring at the table, which made Pete feel very uncomfortable.

"So what now? Do I try to prove that I'm not the villain? Your letter was rather cryptic and the carving a little weird."

"Why don't you start by telling me what you remember about the second day of the hike and the night I disappeared. You see, up till recently, I couldn't remember anything."

"Really? Okay, I'll tell you what I can and Ray, just so you know, I didn't rape anyone!"

A lady seated at a nearby table turned to stare.

"Sorry," Pete said.

"No, I'm sorry. This isn't easy for me either."

Pete lowered his head. "I guess."

"Go ahead," said Ray.

Pete told of their decision to stay at Anderson Pass Camp. How they had enjoyed their evening, but because they couldn't have a campfire, had all turned in early. He slept soundly and was not particularly surprised when he awoke to find Ray out of the tent. Then he related how he, Gordy and Larry started searching for Ray and finally, how he and Larry had gone for help.

"Oh, I almost forgot. Just a minute," Pete said, sliding out of the booth. He walked out the entrance, returning in a minute with a large box. He smiled and handed the box to Ray.

"Here," he said, "it's something I kept. Everything else we gave to your folks."

Ray opened the cardboard box. Inside was his Australian hat.

"Now it's your turn, Ray!"

Both Bill and Sergeant Casper had told Ray not to reveal too much, just enough to see if Pete and the others would slip up and say something that only the one who hit him would know. *This will be tricky*, he thought.

So, without giving any specifics on how he got there, Ray told of how and where Bill O'Hara found him, how he eventually got him to his cave home and how for two years he'd lived with Bill in the backcountry of the Olympic National Park.

"So what makes you think one of us had anything to do with you ending up down the ravine?"

"How else would I have gotten there?"

"Maybe you just slipped and fell."

"No, I didn't just slip and fall."

"You do know how you got there, don't you?" Pete said, his voice echoing his frustration with Ray's vagueness.

"Maybe, but it's still fuzzy. I need to talk to Larry and Gordy and then I have several of appointments with a therapist. He's going to try hypnosis."

"Like you were going to have after we got back from the hike?" Pete asked.

"Yes. Well, I guess that's it for now." Ray hesitated, then reached across the table and offered his hand. Thanks for coming and thanks for bringing my hat."

"You're leaving, just like that! Come on, we were great friends. You can't believe I tried to harm you?"

Ray released Pete's hand and slipped out of the booth. He really didn't think Pete had hit him, but Sergeant Casper had been very clear, "Don't reveal any more than you have to, even though you think the person is innocent. Wait till you've talked to all three and then we'll see what happens."

"There's a pre-rush week party at the fraternity House in two weeks. I'd like to meet you there. Gordy might be back from Spokane by then, too. I'm going to invite Larry and him to join us. I'll tell you all I know then."

"You haven't talked to them yet?"

"No, you're the first." He reached under his jacket and turned off the recorder. "I'll call you next week."

Gordy hadn't been at Spokane's Ridpath Hotel since his East High School's senior prom. The upscale coffee shop was just off the lobby and at first he only saw two customers when he entered. A sign on a metal stand said, "please wait to be seated." He looked at this watch. It was ten before two, so he was early. Then he noticed a third customer, rising from one of the tables at the rear of the shop. It was Ray Wellsford.

"Ray, good to see you again," he said, as he waved and walked back to shake hands. Unlike Pete, Gordy had offered his left hand and positioned his fingers for the secret Xi Alpha grip. Ray had almost forgotten about the "grip" and awkwardly accepted Gordy's hand.

"Oops, I guess I forgot," Ray said.

"That's okay, it's been a while."

"Thanks for coming, Gordy."

"You're kidding, right? Your call and that eerie carving were enough to get me here and after all, we were, and I hope still are, good friends. Jeez, Ray, lighten up."

Without indicating any assent to Gordy's comments, Ray motioned to the seat across from him and sat down. "Last time I saw you, you were limping along."

"Yeah, that's right. That was quite a hike. It didn't end up the way we planned though, did it?"

Ray waved at the waiter.

"I don't know, maybe it did for you."

"Come on, Ray, Shit! You can't think I did anything to cause you to go missing."

The waiter arrived with menus and filled their water glasses.

"Let's order first," said Ray, "and then you can tell me what you remember about our last night and the morning you found me missing. By the way, I don't remember much of anything, so be as detailed as you can."

Gordy didn't appear to pick up on Rays' comment about not remembering and launched into his recollections of the hike and disappearance.

"So you stayed back while Pete and Larry went for help?" Ray said when Gordy was finished. "Interesting. And you recall that Larry climbed down and searched below the moraine?"

"Yes."

Ray sipped at his water and looked directly at Gordy. "I guess it's time to tell you some of what I do remember."

He told him essentially the same story he had told Pete the day before in Seattle. Part way through, the waiter brought them their six-dollar cheeseburgers and fries.

"You lost your memory? Wow. That explains a lot," Gordy said. "This fellow, Bill, he's still living in the cave?"

"No, he's pretty well moved out by now."

"You know, I've always felt guilty that I didn't search more after Larry and Pete left. My leg was still hurting and then it started to snow, but still, I could have at least …"

Ray interrupted him. "No, I understand. You did what you could."

Gordy was silent and nibbled on one of his french fries, which were now cold and soggy. "Then why do you suspect that I could have harmed you? Maybe you just lost your footing and fell over."

"No, I don't think so. Listen, I'd like to get together with you, Pete and Larry in a couple of weeks at the House. There's that pre-rush party and there should be some time when we could get together."

Gordy thought to himself that maybe this meeting today would be the end of it, but obviously, Ray had other ideas. *Damn. That's a couple of weeks earlier than I wanted to go back. If I don't go, I'll look guilty, though.*

"Okay" Gordy said, "any particular time?"

"I'll call you in a couple of days." Ray rose from his chair. "Gordy, I'll get the tab. I really appreciate you meeting me and I hope that after I see Larry and meet with you guys I'll have this all sorted out. At least before they hypnotize me."

"You mean to help you remember how you fell?"

"That and to see if I can shed any light on the rape at the House."

"I thought that was a dead subject."

"No. The cops think that whoever attacked me might be the rapist. I've got to get back," Ray said, this time offering his left hand for the frat grip, leaving his right to press the off button.

―※―

The drive west from Spokane to Yakima was uneventful and Ray pulled into the Best Western Motel parking lot just before six. His dinner meeting with Larry wasn't until seven, so after he checked in, he called Angela and then his folks in Seattle.

Voices from the Mountain

The Red Baron restaurant was packed and he was glad he'd made a reservation. Larry was waiting for him at the check-in stand. He looked older than Ray remembered; perhaps it was his balding head and the long sideburns. His once comical bulldog face was haggard, likely showing the effects of many tough games on the line for Washington. He certainly was heavier, probably close to three hundred pounds, with an ample portion of that weight circling his midsection. Larry had told Ray that the Seahawks training camp was starting in a few days.

Larry spoke first. "Ray, it's great to see you. I'm glad we could get together before I go to Cheney for camp."

"Larry, it's great to see you too," Ray answered, accepting Larry's standard handshake. With a dinner reservation, they were quickly seated. Ray started the recorder.

"Before I ask you some questions, why don't you bring me up to date on what's happening in your life. I suppose being signed by the Seahawks has to top the list?"

While they ordered and started eating, Larry told Ray about his last two years in school and his thrill at being named a second team All-American.

"What about your social life? The last time we were together you were hot and heavy with Karen Simpson."

"We broke up during our junior year. After that, I just played the field. Her friend Ginger got raped and Karen said I wasn't sympathetic. Said I didn't have room for feelings, just for football. I told her Ginger was just a little sex pot."

"Didn't the police think that the person who raped Donna Jones at the dance was the same one that raped Ginger?"

"Yes, but I think she wiggled her little butt once too often."

Ray squirmed at that comment. His friend had gotten more callous than he remembered. "Why don't you tell me about the hike two years ago and what you remember when I came up missing."

Larry told much the same story as Pete and Gordy. When asked about climbing down the moraine, he didn't remember doing so and thought maybe it was Pete.

"So what did happen to you? You can't believe one of us had anything to do with it. You must have slipped off the edge."

"Not exactly. You see, I didn't remember a great deal of anything until a few weeks ago. That's why I'm talking to each of you. Somebody knows something they're not telling."

"Hell, Ray, we were good buddies. Come on, you know more than you're telling me."

"Not really." Then hesitantly, "Who do you think may have tried to kill me? Which face should be carved?"

Larry just shook his head. Ray sat unmoving, staring at Larry until he broke the silence.

"Listen, I'd like to meet with you, Gordy and Pete at the alumni pre-rush party at the House in a couple of weeks. I'll have more to tell you then. I'd really appreciate it if you can come. I know it's during your football camp, but just one day is all I ask."

"I don't know," Larry said.

"Don't say no now, I'll call you in a few days."

"Okay, I don't have the phone number in Cheney, but call my mom. It would be great to have the old Motley Crew back together again."

As Ray watched Larry leave he thought, *of the three, he's the likely candidate.*

When Ray got to his room he called Sergeant Casper.

Replays and Discovery

They'd been listening to the tapes in Casper's office for over an hour. Ray was tired. It had been a long drive back from Yakima that morning and an accident on the Lake Washington floating bridge didn't help. Traffic was gridlocked on I-90 several miles east of the I-405 Interchange, making him almost an hour late. The tape of his meeting with Larry was just finishing.

"Interesting," Casper said, stopping the tape and hitting the rewind button.

"Is that it, just interesting? I took a big chance taping those conversations, you know."

"No, sorry, it was more than interesting. I'm just puzzled. What did you think?"

Ray thought about that for a moment. "I guess I'd have to say that other than the confusion about who climbed down the moraine, their stories were about the same."

"Did it give you any clues to which one hit you?"
"No."
"I agree, there's nothing in the tapes that seems to incriminate any of them," Casper said.
"Should I still go ahead and call them all about getting together at the fraternity House?"
"Yes, and I'll listen to the tapes again and call you, Ray."

The meeting at the fraternity House was well attended by both alumni and "actives." Two dates for late summer rush parties were selected and incoming senior, Al Stocker, was selected for rush chairman. Ray handled all the questions about his disappearance and resurfacing as best he could. It got old real fast, but he realized everyone was curious. It was especially good to see some of his closer friends: Cloyd Carson, Hank Mason, Al Stocker, and, as promised in their phone conversations, Larry, Pete and Gordy.

When the meeting ended in the Chapter Room, everyone congregated in the dining hall for drinks and a buffet. It had been obvious to Ray from the onset that he wouldn't be able to privately talk with anyone until later that evening, so he, Gordy, Pete and Larry were going to meet at Ingram's on Roosevelt after the buffet.

Ray spotted Pete and Hank in the beer line and Hank motioned to him. Hank appeared to have had several beers.

"You're getting to be quite the celebrity, Ray," Hank said, as Ray approached. "Come on, join us."

"Thanks." He'd only talked briefly to Hank and was curious to hear if he had anything to add to the other's stories.

"I heard you're staying at your folks?" Hank said.

"Just temporarily. I think I'll finish out the summer in Amanda Park and then move to Queen Anne this fall when school starts."

"You're going back to school?" Pete asked.

"Thinking about it."

"Pete tells me you're still trying to figure out what happened to you on the hike two years ago. I can't believe you think one of them crept out and cold cocked you," Hank said.

"Well, someone did, but, you're right, I am having a hard time with the idea." He paused and nodded to Pete. "Hopefully, by tomorrow I'll know a little more."

Al Stocker joined in and the conversation shifted to whether the Huskies would be good enough to win the conference and get to the Rose Bowl. Ray switched off the recorder.

They'd been sitting at a table in the rear of the Ingram's Tavern, nursing their beers for ten minutes and from the conversation so far, Ray had learned nothing new. In fact, he was more and more convinced that he and Casper must be wrong about Pete, Larry or Gordy's complicity. He left the recorder on, but relaxed for the first time that day. *Maybe I've had too much beer*, he thought. Pete must have thought the same.

"Ray, you seem like your old self tonight," Pete said.

"You think so, huh?" Ray raised his glass. "To the Motley Crew."

Larry was the first to suggest it was time to call it a day. "Listen, guys, it's getting late. I have to leave Pete and Betty's place real early to get home tomorrow."

"Larry's right. Besides, I told Betty we'd be home early. Ray, I don't know what else I can tell you."

"I know," said Ray, "let's call it a night. Thank you guys. Maybe after my hypnosis therapy I'll have some answers."

"Are you staying in town tonight, Ray"? Gordy asked.

"Yes, and for the next three days. Then back to the Peninsula for the weekend."

They all shook hands and Pete even gave Ray a hug. "We're glad you're back with us. Let's stay in touch," Pete said, releasing his grip and looking directly at Ray.

"Thanks, all of you," said Ray. "This has really meant a lot to me and I will keep in touch."

As Ray drove his dad's car south on Aurora he thought about his day and replayed in his mind the conversations he'd had. In total, he felt he had learned little of value in solving the mystery of his attack and the identity of the attacker. His first appointment with a Dr. Schlossburg was in two days.

His dad met him at the door. "Ray, you got a call from Angela." He looked at his watch. "She'll be there for another ten minutes. She sure was excited. Says she's found something real fascinating."

Ray dialed the Rhodes' Portland number he was getting to know by heart. Angela's dad answered on the second ring. "Hello."

"Mr. Rhodes, hi. This is Ray. Angela called earlier."

"Hello, Ray. Just a minute, she's upstairs finishing her packing."

Ray tried to imagine what Angela had to tell him that was so important. She was leaving tomorrow for Lynnfield and her last semester, but that he already knew.

"Ray," she sounded out of breath.

"Hi," he said. "What's got you gulping for air?"

Without so much as a brief howdy do, Angela launched into her story.

That afternoon she had gone to Bartell Drug to get a few last minute items for school. As she was leaving she passed the sign announcing the "Employee of the Month" and was stopped dead in her tracks. The photograph was of someone she'd either seen before, or the resemblance was uncannily similar. Then she looked at the name. It was Lan Thi. She instantly remembered where she'd seen the face of the oriental girl before. Bill O'Hara's drawings in the cave.

Ray had to interrupt. "That's impossible. Bill's sure she died that night in the Drung village. Must just be a really weird coincidence."

"No, I tell you, it's her. Think! Same first name and same face. Maybe a little older looking, but definitely the same face."

"You didn't get to meet her?" Ray asked.

"No. She works nights, Wednesday through Sunday."

"Did you get her phone number or address?"

"No. The store won't give out that information. All I did is leave my folk's number, but I'm leaving first thing in the morning. If she doesn't call before I leave, I'll call Bartells and give them your number. Okay?"

Ray wasn't so sure if it was okay or not. Vietnamese must have similar first names just like Americans do, but he couldn't discount the picture. Then, too, Angela had only briefly seen Bill's drawing.

"Yes, okay, I guess. I'm not going to call Bill and get him excited until I talk to her. That is, if she even calls."

"I can tell you're not convinced, but just go along with me on this, Ray."

"All right." *She hasn't even asked about my day and the meeting with Pete, Larry and Gordy*, he thought.

As if reading his mind, she said, "Okay, your turn! What's been going on and do you think you're any closer to figuring everything out?"

Ray told her of the meeting at the Chapter House and then his short time with the three guys at the tavern.

"So, you really don't know anything more?"

"No. Well, maybe. I just don't think any of them did it. Sergeant Casper is still reviewing all the tapes from before and I'll give him the ones from today, but I think it's a dead end."

"When's your appointment with the psychologist?"

"Day after tomorrow."

Ray was struggling to find the words he wanted to say to Angela. It was something he'd wanted to say for some time. "Angela?"

"Yes, Ray." She heard the hesitation in his voice and knew him enough to know he was anxious.

"I'll miss you. I ah ... can't wait to see you again."

"I'll miss you too, Ray. I've got a couple days off in two weeks. How about I meet you in Amanda Park?"

"I'd love that. I'll call you if I end up hearing from the girl."

"Bye, Ray, I lo…" But he was gone.

The ringing of the telephone interrupted breakfast at the Wellsford's. Ray's mom handed him the phone.

"It's Sergeant Casper."

Ray listened as Casper told him of a rape committed in University District the previous night. A high school girl was walking along 15th NE when she was pulled into an alley and sexually assaulted. The girl was beat up, but survived. When questioned she remembered that her assailant called her a dirty slut and smelled of alcohol and cologne. She remembered the cologne because her older brother's had the same musky smell.

"Sounds just like what Donna Jones told you two years ago," said Ray.

"Yes it does, and much like the rape on campus later that September."

"So you think it's the same person?"

"I do. I also think that it's the guy that hit you and I'll bet that seeing you again somehow triggered his action."

"One of my fraternity brothers, you mean?"

"Yes. It's too much of a coincidence," Casper said.

"Maybe. By the way, I've got the tape from last night and I'll drop it by on my way to the doctor's office."

The first session with Dr. Jules Schlossburg lasted less than an hour. Mostly Ray filled out forms in the outer office and then with the doctor, answered questions about his family, his two years at Washington, and the hike. The subject of Bill O'Hara and his life in the Olympics was left for another time.

Ray guessed Schlossburg was in his forties, maybe early fifties. He was graying at the temples and his half frame reading glasses rested low on his Roman nose.

The doctor's private office wall was papered with diplomas and award certificates. His desk was almost empty save for a pen and pencil set, a single pipe in a stand and two spiral notebooks. There had been three, but one was now in use, as Schlossburg seemed to be writing down everything Ray said.

"I think that's enough for now. Same time on Friday and we'll talk about the hypnosis and maybe give it a try. Oh, and bring the journals from the cave with you." Schlossburg rose from his red leather chair, closed the notebook and smiled. "Any questions?"

"No. Not yet, anyway. I'm on my way to see Sergeant Casper."

"Fine. I talked to him this morning and he's hoping that our sessions will eventually help you remember more and especially about the night you were attacked."

Schlossburg came around his desk and opened the office door for Ray. "See you Friday, then."

Sergeant Casper had to leave on another case, so Ray left the tape for him and headed home. His dad met him at the door.

"We're getting to be your answering service, Ray."

"What?"

"Just kidding, son. You got a call from a Lan Thi. Sounded oriental. She left her number and will be there till six."

Ray took the piece of paper from his dad. *Well, here goes,* he thought. *It's just got to be a mistake. But then, why would she call back?*

The phone was answered on the second ring. "Hello."

"My name's Ray Wellsford. My friend Angela tried to call you."

"Yes." Then silence.

"Is this Lan Thi?" No answer.

"Hello?"

"My name is Lan. How can I help you?" As his dad had said, she spoke in broken English with a definite oriental quality.

Ray decided not to beat around the bush and launched right into it. "I have a friend named Bill O'Hara who served in Viet Nam. Do you know him?"

He heard a sudden intake of breath, then deafening silence.

"Are you still there?"

Voices from the Mountain

"That's impossible. The Bill O'Hara I know is ..." She didn't finish. " This is a cruel joke Who is this?"

"Ray Wellsford. It's not a joke. I live in Washington State and ..."

Before he could finish he heard a sob and then she hung up. *What to do? Should he call back? Could she really be Bill's Lan?*

As he contemplated these questions, the phone rang. "I'll get it he yelled," thinking it was the girl calling back.

It was Sergeant Casper. "Ray, I got the tape. Thanks, I'll listen to it tonight before I leave work."

"Good. I'll be here a couple more days then I'm heading back to Amanda Park for a while. Bill said he was going to get a phone, so you can get the number through information. I'll be staying with him."

"Anything else I should know about?"

"No, not really."

"Okay, call me when you're back in Seattle and I'll call you if there's anything on the new tapes. And Ray, I'm worried this guy is going to rape again, and if he thinks you can identify him, he may come after you once more."

―――

It was a dark, dreary day and the clouds hung low over Puget Sound, obscuring any view beyond the tops of the buildings that lined First and Second Avenues. Dr. Schlossburg had just finished explaining the technique he used when hypnotizing a patient. Schlossburg used a fairly common method that involved eye fixation: the patient is asked to fixate his eyes on an object while the doctor suggests the eyes are becoming heavy and are closing. Then, in the case of Ray, he will try to get him to recall the scene the night of the rape at the Xi Alpha House. If Ray is susceptible, Schlossburg will also attempt to get Ray to recall any additional details about the night he was attacked.

"So, you want to give it a try? I'll just ask some general questions to see if you're going to be a good subject. Then next visit, we'll get specific about the night of the rape."

Ray wasn't so sure he wanted to do it. He'd heard some stories about people doing strange things when they're put under.

"What happens if I don't wake up? I mean, what if something happens to you while I'm hypnotized?"

"You'll always wake up. Also, I can't make you do anything you don't want to do. Deep down if you want to recall the incident, you will. If you don't at first we'll go deeper, but nothing happens without your consent."

"Okay. Let's give it a go."

Dr. Schlossburg had Ray use the recliner on the other side of the office, removed a crystal pendant from his desk and sat in the chair next to Ray. "Let your body calm down, unwind."

Ray relaxed and concentrated on the slowly swinging pendant and Schlossburg's voice. He was tired. *Rest ---hmmm.*

"Ray! Come on, wake up. That's it for today."

"What? I didn't go to sleep?"

"No, quite the contrary. You did great. I think it will be just fine. We'll get started in earnest next week."

Ray was glad he was spending the weekend with Bill in Amanda Park. He felt guilty, however, borrowing his dad's car again. Hank Mason had said anytime Ray needed a ride to give him a call, but Ray didn't want to impose. Hank was working in the accounting department at the mill in Forks, about an hour's drive north of Amanda Park.

He didn't try to call Angela before he left, but would when he got to Bill's. He needed to tell her about his failed attempt to communicate with the person that Angela was convinced was Lan Thi. How he would do that without Bill overhearing would be another problem.

It proved to be no problem, for as soon as Ray arrived, Bill left for the store after telling Ray to go ahead and call Angela. Ray was surprised when Angela answered on the first ring. In no time he told her of his short conversation with Lan Thi.

"I don't think we ought to forget about it, Ray. If need be I'll drive to her work and confront her."

"So you really still think she's Bill's Lan?"

"I'm not sure, but the only way we'll know is to see her."

"All right." Through the cabin window he could see Bill approaching. "Bill's coming so I'd better change the subject."

When Bill entered, Ray was asking Angela about her classes and how soon they might see each other.

"Say hello for me," Bill said quietly.

The decor of Bill's cabin wasn't much different than that of his cave home: a narrow wooden bed, a storage cabinet in much need of paint, and an overflowing bookcase. However, a chest high workbench took the place of his rickety table and a new wood stove had been a welcome substitute for the fire pit.

"So how's Angela?"

"Fine and she says hello, too." Ray wished he could say more, but until Angela talked to Lan Thi, he could not.

"How did your meetings with your friends go and the sessions with the doctor?"

Ray missed his long discussions with Bill and was eager to unload all the events of the past several days.

Orchid Flower

Angela borrowed her roommate's car to make the hour's drive from Lynnfield to Portland and the Bartells Drug where Lan Thi was employed. As far as she had been able to determine, Lan was working this evening.

The poster showing Lan Thi as the Employee of the Month was still tacked to the entryway bulletin board. Angela took another look. She scanned the checkout counters and down the nearest aisle and didn't see anyone that looked like the picture. Then she spotted her. She was behind the photo department counter. *Well, here goes nothing*, she thought.

No one was waiting for help, so Angela walked right up to the counter. "Hello."

The woman, who was putting photo envelopes in a file drawer, looked up. "Yes, may I help you?"

Angela hesitated. The likeness was uncanny. Her company photograph didn't do her justice. She was strikingly beautiful.

Her radiant black hair was cut in a bob that framed a classic oval face. Either Bill had an incredible memory or Lan had a twin sister. She offered her hand and smiled, but the offered hand was not taken.

"I'm Angela, we talked over the phone," was all she could think to say.

The once cheerful smile disappeared and the woman looked like she was going to bolt and run.

"Please, give me a few minutes to explain," Angela said.

"All right." She seemed to relax. "Let me ask the manager if I can take a break."

As the woman walked from behind the counter, Angela noticed she had a slight limp. *She looks about the right age*, Angela thought, *probably mid-twenties*.

She returned in a minute and motioned for Angela to follow. "We'll go in the break room."

As soon as they entered, the woman turned to Angela. "I am sorry that I was impolite to you and your friend that called." She indicated a chair for Angela and sat in one opposite.

"My name is Lan Thi and I did know a Bill O'Hara in Viet Nam."

So there it was, thought Angela. *Now, where to start?* But, she didn't have to worry. Lan continued ...

"You say you know Bill O'Hara. That means he is still alive, yes?"

"Yes, he is very much alive and living only a few hours north of here in Washington."

Lan sat very still and then her lip began to tremble and Angela saw tears running down her face.

"If only you knew how I had searched for him. I finally gave up, believing he was probably dead."

"He thinks you're dead," said Angela, now firmly believing that she had found Bill's Lan. "Why don't you tell me about what happened in Viet Nam and how you got here?"

"I should get back to work, but it's quiet tonight and if the manager will let me off early, we can go next door to the coffee shop."

Angela nodded as Lan hurriedly left and just as fast, returned. "Yes, I have the rest of my shift off."

They sat opposite each other in the small café and without preamble, Lan told her story.

When the North Vietnamese Army attack began on the Drung village, Lan had not yet reached the hut she shared with Bill. As the mortars fell around her, she dropped the water jug and ran to rocks that bordered the edge of the village. Just before she reached cover, a mortar fell near her and she felt a sharp pain in her leg. She realized she'd been hit, but despite the pain, Lan continued on until she found shelter under a large rock beyond the perimeter of the village.

Lying there, she heard, rather than saw, the NVA soldiers charge the village, the sounds of their weapons discharging, the screams and then the crackling of the fires that consumed her home. Fearing she might still be found when it got light, she rolled from beneath the rock and moved stealthily away from the village. How far she went she didn't know, but eventually was overcome by the pain of her wound and finding a trench-like depression, crawled in and fell asleep.

She awoke to silence. The crude bandage she'd fashioned from her shirt had stopped the bleeding, but infection would soon set in. That, plus another night of mountain temperatures would take their toll if she didn't find better shelter, some food and water.

Voices from the Mountain

Part of her wanted to go back to the village and see if Bill and her family had survived, but instead, she forced herself to walk further away and east toward another village where she hoped she could find help. A mile or so from where she thought the village was, she reached a creek. While she was kneeling down to drink, she heard a noise behind her. It was two men and a woman.

Their village too had been attacked. Fortunately for Lan, they had food, soap and a sterile dressing. Lan's saga of the next several weeks was sketchy, but Angela gathered that the four Drung joined more survivors and made their way south, eventually getting to the port of Thuy Hoa on the China Sea. Lan stayed there until the NVA overran Hue and Da Nang.

"What did you do then?" Angela asked when Lan stopped her narrative momentarily.

"We did the same foolish thing that many did, and died trying."

"What's that?"

"We made a raft and set out to sea." She continued her tale.

When Da Nang fell they knew the communists would be moving swiftly south toward Saigon and their only chance was taking to the sea, hoping that the Americans would find them. They were lucky. A month later, Lan was one of several thousand refugees at a camp in Guam. In 1976 she was fortunate to be in a group that was moved to a resettlement camp in California.

At the camp she went through a six-month school that prepared her for entry into American society. Then in early 1977 she was sponsored by a church in Sacramento and began her life in the United States. Through a Vietnamese refugee organization, Lan learned that her aunt and uncle were part of a large Vietnamese community in Portland, Oregon, and she moved there in late 1977.

Once she was established and had a job, she traveled to the Seattle area and began her search in hopes that Bill O'Hara was still alive and had returned home. Lan told how she found out that Bill had survived the war, had worked at Boeing and then where he had lived, but the trail abruptly ended. No one had seen or heard of Bill O'Hara since November of 1977.

Lan made additional trips to Washington well into 1978 — all dead ends. One friend from Boeing did tell her that Bill had seemed very depressed the last time he saw him, even talking of suicide. Eventually she gave up hope and focused on her life in Portland.

Lan looked at Angela and nodded her head, as if to signal, "Now it's your turn."

Angela didn't know many of the details, but recalling what Ray told her, and her time with Bill, she did the best she could.

Lan slowly shook her head when Angela finished.

"He has been living in the mountains for three years?"

"Yes, and for almost the past two, with my friend Ray."

"He thinks I'm dead." It wasn't really a question, but Angela nodded.

"He hasn't forgotten you, though. His cave home was filled with sketches of you and when he talks about your life together in Viet Nam, you can hear the emotion in his voice. If I hadn't seen the one drawing of you, I would have never recognized you from the picture at your work."

"You say, was filled. Has he moved?"

"Yes, to a cabin in the town of Amanda Park. It's on the edge of the Olympic National Forest, near Lake Quinault."

"Have you told him about me yet?"

"No."

"Your friend, Ray, where is he now?"

"Maybe I'd better tell you about how Ray came to be with Bill. It explains a lot of the reasons why Bill stayed so long in the mountains and why he left."

They ordered tomato soup and toasted cheese sandwiches and Angela told Lan about Ray Wellsford.

When she was finished, Lan smiled. "I can tell that he is more than just a friend, as you put it."

"Well, maybe, but right now I'm in school and he's trying to find out who tried to kill him. Not a good time for romance."

"Will your Ray now tell Bill about me?"

"That's up to you."

Lan Thi bowed her head and started to cry. "It's been so long. I am not the same person he once loved. My leg ... ah."

"I think your leg will make little difference to him, Lan."

"Then please have Ray tell him that I am alive." She sighed and took a piece of paper from her purse. "Here's the phone number at my apartment."

Realizing it was getting late, both Angela and Lan rose and then awkwardly but without hesitation, hugged each other.

"Thank you," they said, almost in unison.

"I'll call Ray when I get back to Lynnfield."

Lost Love

Ray was packing for the trip back to Seattle when Bill's phone rang. It was Angela. He listened without interruption as she told of her meeting with Lan Thi.

"She's had quite a life and is very eager to see Bill," Angela said as she finished.

"Bill's not here, by the way."

"Is he at the store?"

"No. Believe it or not, he decided to make a last trip back to the cave. Seems he forgot something."

"When's he due back?"

"Late tomorrow, and I've got to leave here in an hour or so."

They discussed their options and decided that Ray would leave a note for Bill to call him at his folk's in Seattle. Angela would call Lan and let her know what was going on, and not expect to hear anything for a day or so.

"Is your next doctor's appointment on Monday?"

"No, Tuesday. On Monday night I'm going to the Seahawks pre-season game at the Kingdome. Pete got tickets and a bunch of us are meeting at McCormick's after the game."

"Have fun. Doesn't sound like you miss me at all," Angela said. "Just kidding."

⁂

He watched the two women walk to the parking garage. He'd been following them ever since they left the bar and headed up First Avenue. Staying in the shadows he saw the short one wave and open the door to the stairs to the upper floor. He wasn't interested in her, anyway. He much preferred the taller blond one that had caught his eye in McCormick's.

She walked to a dark Chevy coupe and reached in her purse.

He hesitated. *Better wait to see if the other one comes down.* He was thinking he'd probably lost his chance when a Ford Fairlane came down the ramp and slowed down by the Chevy. He crouched down and listened.

"You okay?" said the one in the Ford.

"Yes, go ahead. I couldn't find my keys. Got it unlocked now, and I'll just get in and let it warm up a little while. See you tomorrow."

"You're sure. It's pretty deserted?"

"No, it's fine. I'll be okay."

"All right. See you at work."

The Ford accelerated and drove down the ramp to the exit. As it did, he heard the Chevy engine start and turned to look in that direction. *It was now or never.* The excitement of the impending encounter always aroused him.

He removed the small bottle of cologne from his coat and dabbed some on. The musky smell never failed to heighten his desire. Rising, he walked unsteadily toward the Chevy, a set of keys dangling from his hand. To an observer, he looked like someone who'd had one drink too many trying to find his car. It was a scam he'd used before.

Just in front of the car, he stumbled and fell. His action had the desired effect. The girl opened her car door.

"Are you all right?" she called.

"I'm not sure." He pretended to try and rise, supporting himself on the front of the car. "Sorry about that."

She turned off the car and got out. "Here, let me help."

He grabbed her offered hand and swiftly clamped his other around her mouth, pushing her face down beside the car.

"Just be quiet you little bitch and you'll be all right!"

She didn't heed the warning, tried to scream through his fingers and struggled to get out of his grip. He released the hand on her mouth and slapped her, but in so doing she was able to see his face. He forced her down again on her stomach and tried to pull her pants down. She twisted from side to side and he punched her with his fist. Hard! She lay still.

Ray overslept and was ten minutes late for his appointment. Dr. Schlossburg seemed not to mind and opening one of his ever-present note pads, began their third session with no prologue.

"Any new memories?"

"No."

"All right, let's try the hypnosis and see what we can learn," Schlossburg said, while at the same time removing the crystal pendant from his desk drawer.

Ray was a good subject and in no time, Schlossburg was able to probe deeper than he had before. He started with the night of the rape at the fraternity House. Choosing his questions carefully, he brought Ray through the circumstances of the evening and eventually to the scene in the second floor hallway.

"Ray. The person you saw in the hallway, was it a male?"

"Yes."

"Did you know the person?"

"I'm not sure ... no ... I, ah,"

"Because it was dark?"

"Yes."

Dr. Schlossburg tried several lead-in approaches to try and get Ray to describe the person he saw, but whenever he got too specific, Ray was not able to offer any details. The questioning went on for another ten minutes and then Schlossburg brought Ray back.

"Anything?" Ray asked.

"Not anything about the assailant. I'm beginning to think that you really didn't see enough to identify the person. He must think so, though, or he wouldn't have tried to kill you on the hike."

"So it must be either Pete, Larry, or Gordy, then?"

"I would think so. It doesn't make sense unless one of them had other reasons to attack you." He closed his notepad. "On Thursday we'll concentrate on the hike and see if that leads us somewhere."

Dr. Schlossburg buzzed his receptionist, Mrs. Davis, to let her know the session had ended. As Ray got up, there was a knock at the door and Mrs. Davis entered. "Doctor, I have a message for Mr. Wellsford. He's to call Sergeant Casper before he leaves."

"You can call from here, Ray," Schlossburg offered, getting up and motioning to his desk.

Ray dialed the number and shortly Casper came on the line. Jules Schlossburg watched Ray's expression change from anticipatory to grim, signaling that it wasn't good news. Ray hung up.

"There was another rape last night and this time the victim was killed," Ray said, looking very dejected.

"They think it was the same person?"

"Yes, and the girl's body was found next to her car in the parking garage, just two blocks from McCormick's."

"Where you were last night?" Schlossburg asked.

"Yes."

"Who else was there from your crowd?" Casper asked.

"Just about all of our pledge class." He paused. "I've got to go. See you on Thursday. If I hear anything, I'll let you know."

"Be careful, Ray, he's getting more violent."

Ray's dad greeted him at the door. "Bill called. He's back at the cabin."

Ray realized that he had little choice but to tell Bill about Lan Thi. He wished he could do it face-to-face, but didn't have that luxury. He almost hoped that Bill wouldn't answer, but he did, on the second ring.

"How was your trip back to the cave?" was all he could think to say.

"Just fine. I may have to go back one more time and then that will be it, but that can't be why you wanted me to call. Your note sounded more urgent than that."

Ray was uncertain how to begin, then —"You know they always say to the person that's going to be told something surprising to sit down. Are you sitting?"

"No," he laughed, " but go ahead. Come on, Ray, what is it?"

"Angela and I have discovered that Lan Thi is alive and living in Portland!" There it was. He just blurted it out.

Silence doesn't adequately describe the next few seconds. It was like Ray remembered when he'd camped near a lake one Spring. At night the frogs would chatter away and then suddenly there was total quiet.

"Bill, Bill, are you there?"

"I'm here. How do you know for sure?"

"Angela met with her a few days ago."

More silence. Ray figured he might as well tell what he had learned and then let Bill go from there. "I'll tell you what I know."

Ray started with the call from Angela about the poster in Bartell Drug, then the ensuing calls, and finally the meeting in Portland.

"And she thought I was dead, too. My God, after all these years and she's just a couple hundred miles away."

"If you've got a pencil handy, I'll give you her number."

Bill's hand shook as he wrote down the number, said goodbye to Ray, and hung up. He realized that he hadn't even asked about how Ray was doing. *How ironical*, he thought, *I return from the cave with some sketches of Lan that I forgot, and find out she's alive.* He looked at the paper in his hand. *Should I call now?* He still couldn't believe it. *Would she still want him?* He picked up the phone and dialed.

"Hello?"

It was her! "Lan, this is Bill."

"Bill. Oi troi phat oi!"

He remembered that what she said was something like, "Oh my God" in Vietnamese.

"Yes, it's me. I … ah," he just couldn't think what to say. Then, "Lan, I thought you were dead. I mean the hut was destroyed. I looked for you. Oh God, I missed you so."

"I too. I, … have always thought about you. I looked for you in Washington."

"Yes, I know, Ray told me. I've got to see you."

"Can you come here?"

"I don't have a car, but probably can borrow one. Tomorrow's Wednesday, let's see …"

Lan interrupted his thought. "Angela said she would go with me on the bus this weekend."

Bill thought about that. Ray wouldn't be back till late Friday with a car. That was only two days.

"If I can borrow a car from here I will, or I can wait till Ray gets back. I'll see. Maybe it will be better for you to come on Saturday. I'll call you tomorrow."

Their conversation continued for several more minutes. Finally Bill had to say what he'd wanted to say from the very beginning. "Lan, I love you."

"I love you, too, Bill. I always have."

A Narrowed Focus

Ray spent most of Wednesday at the University firming up his class schedule for the Fall Quarter. He was determined to pick up where he left off in 1978 and hopefully, get his degree in less than two years. His major had been Business Administration, with a minor in Marketing. Now he was thinking seriously of switching to Forestry, but he'd have to see how many of his credits would transfer.

When he finished with the Business Department counselor it was only two, so Ray decided to stop by the police station. If he could see Casper today, maybe he could leave for Amanda Park right after his appointment with Dr. Schlossburg.

Casper was in. "Ray, I'm glad you came today. I need you to be a bit more specific on who was with you at McCormick's."

Ray thought for a moment. "Let's see, at first there was Pete, Gordy, Cloyd, Ben Simons, Hank and Al. Then Larry joined us a few minutes later.

"Larry played in the game?"

"Yes. For most of the last quarter."

"Did you all leave together?"

"Pretty much. Everyone had his own car except Al Stocker. Oh, I remember now, Larry did leave first. He had to go back to the stadium to catch the team bus back to Cheney."

"Who was Al with?"

"He was riding with Ben Simons."

"Okay, thanks. Call me before you head back to the coast."

After Ray left, Casper sat silently in his chair looking out his sixth floor window at the raindrops hitting the cement sill. It hadn't been the typical Seattle summer; well below average rainfall. The natives would characteristically say, "We need the rain."

Everything about this case just didn't add up. There had been four rapes over a two-year period. The last one ending up in a murder. On at least three of the occasions, he knew someone from Ray's crowd was close at hand. The rapist's face had never been seen. That is until the other night, he guessed. Perhaps Ray had seen the attacker, but the doctor had so far been unable to get Ray to remember.

Casper reasoned the guilty party was one of Ray's three close friends, especially considering the attack on the hike. *Damn*, he thought, *what am I missing?* There's just no obvious pattern, no clues except perhaps the musk cologne and the rapist's calling the women a bitch. "Nothing!" he said out loud. He decided he would listen to all the tapes one more time. *There's got to be something I'm overlooking.*

Ray too thought about the rapes and the murder as he drove to his folk's home on Queen Anne Hill. He still couldn't accept that Pete, Gordy or Larry might be the culprit. The discovery of Lan Thi and his growing relationship with Angela had consumed his thoughts of late, but he realized that he should take Casper's warning seriously.

Ray's dad met him at the door. "Well, this is getting to be a habit. Your mother and I feel like we're the Ray Wellsford answering service." Then he broke into a smile. "Just kidding, son. We're happy to have you here." He handed Ray a piece of paper. "Angela called about an hour ago. Here's the number."

Angela had good news. Bill and Lan had talked. She was trying to help Lan get to Amanda Park. Bill was trying to borrow a car. His other choice was to wait until Ray got back late Friday.

As Angela talked, Ray had an idea. Hank Mason lived in Forks. *Maybe?*

"Could the two of you get to Forks by bus?"

"I think so. I'm sure we can get a ride to the bus station in Portland, but that still doesn't get us to Amanda Park without either you or Bill picking us up."

"You've heard me mention one of my fraternity friends, Hank Mason?"

"Yes."

"He lives in Forks and offered a couple of times to help out with transportation. I'm sure he'd be glad to meet you guys and drive you to Amanda Park."

"That would be great," she said. "Let me call Lan and see when she can get away and I'll check my class schedule and the bus schedule. This Thursday night would be the earliest."

"All right, I'll call Bill and then call Hank and get back to you. I think it may work out, especially since I can't get the car until late Friday."

"Ray, this is fantastic. I know Lan will be excited and I am too."

"Oh, is that so." He sniggered.

"Easy boy!"

"All right, bye for now."

Ray didn't seen to be his normally cheerful self.

"You look a bit frazzled today," Dr. Schlossburg said, as he closed the inner-office door and walked around Ray to sit down. "Coffee or water?"

"No, nothing, thanks. I just have a lot on my mind. I wanted to leave for Amanda Park after our session today, but dad's car won't be available until late tomorrow."

"Why?"

"Needed some work, I guess. I don't know," he said, sounding impatient. "It all worked out, though. I'll tell you later."

Schlossburg said, "Let's get started then."

Ray shrugged his shoulders and sat down.

"As I said last time, I want to focus on the hike today."

"You're going to put me under again?"

"Yes," he said, pulling out the now familiar pendant.

Ray relaxed and with practiced efficiency, Dr. Schlossburg had him in a deep sleep in just a few minutes.

Schlossburg asked a few general questions and then zeroed in on the night at Mt. Anderson Pass Camp.

"Ray, what did you have for dinner that night?"

"Beef stroganoff."

Four questions later he started homing in. "Tell me about when you climbed out of the tent to relieve yourself."

Ray told the story that he'd relived in his mind many times. The incident he finally remembered when he and Bill had gone to the Pass camp. However, when he got to the point where someone hit him, he hesitated.

"You heard a noise and then you turned?" Schlossburg prompted.

"Yes."

"Go on, Ray. What happened next?"

Voices from the Mountain

"I thought it was an animal and then I saw that it was, ah ... I ..."

"What, Ray. Did you see the person's face?"

"No," sounding very emphatic.

Ray started to fidget in his chair and then he started trembling. *Time to stop*, thought Schlossburg. *He's likely remembering being hit and falling.* He brought Ray quickly out of the trance.

"That's it for today," Schlossburg said when Ray was fully awake.

"Anything new?"

"No, not really. We've had five sessions and I think one more might do it. Say next Tuesday. I'll call Sergeant Casper and bring him up to date, but frankly, I think you just didn't see the face of your attacker."

"I guess not," Ray said.

"What are your plans for this weekend? You seemed a wee bit frazzled when you arrived today."

Ray told Schlossburg how he had gotten hold of Hank Mason and that he'd agreed to meet Angela and Lan Thi in Forks and take them to Amanda Park. How he'd called Bill and let him know. Then he told the additional good news that solved all his problems.

"My friend Pete called this morning to see how I was doing and he's got Friday off and he's going to take me to Amanda Park. I don't have to wait till later to go."

"That's great. Your dad's probably happy to have his car this weekend." He opened his top desk drawer, removed a leather pouch and reached for his pipe.

"I'm supposed to call Sergeant Casper in the morning, and then I'm on my way."

"All right then, see you next week."

Pete Fairchild knocked on the Wellsford's door just after nine. Ray could tell right away that he was agitated about something. Pete's face always got beet red and his freckles seemed to double in number when he was under stress.

"You're late," Ray said. "The traffic must have been bad, you look like you're ready to explode."

"The traffic wasn't that bad, just got into a little tiff with Betty before I left."

"Hope it didn't have anything to do with you taking me?"

"No, something else. Anyway, I'm starved. What's for breakfast?" quickly changing the subject.

Janice and Tom Wellsford came in from the other room. "Pete, good to see you again," they said, almost in unison.

"Mom, would you please get this starving guy something to eat. I need to finish packing, so we can get going."

They heard the phone ringing as they walked back up the front porch steps. "I'll get it," Tom Wellsford said, quickening his pace.

It was Detective Sergeant Casper.

"Mr. Wellsford, I need to talk to Ray right away."

"He just left."

"He was supposed to call me. I thought he wasn't leaving until later?"

Tom told him how Hank had agreed to meet the girls and drive them to Amanda Park, and then that Ray got the offer from Pete, so he could leave early.

"Oh, my God! I've got to get a hold of him," Casper said.

Revelation

Sergeant Casper hung up the phone. "Damn!"

He'd listened to Ray's secretly recorded tapes once again the day before, still hoping he'd missed a detail that would help identify the attacker. Then at home last night he remembered something that seemed odd and had rushed into work to replay one of the tapes this morning.

Casper rewound the tape from the fraternity pre-rush party. How had he missed it? It was there all the time. He now was convinced that he at least knew who had attacked Ray on the hike. *Was that person also the rapist? What other motive would he have?*

Frustrated that he'd missed Ray, he called Bill's number in Amanda Park. He let it ring for over a minute, but no one answered. He decided to wait awhile and try Bill's number again. He needed to warn Ray, and quickly.

The bus from Portland pulled into the small station in Forks at just after one p.m., about a half hour early. Angela had dozed off a few times, as had Lan, but for the most part they'd enjoyed sharing more of their life stories and talking about Bill and Ray.

Angela hadn't met Hank Mason but had a good idea what he looked like from Ray's description. She needn't have worried however, for when they climbed down the exit steps, someone, whom she concluded was Hank, was standing with a sign that in large letters said, "Angela and Lan."

"Hi, I'm Hank. Great to meet you both."

"Thanks," Angela said. Lan smiled and nodded.

"Let's get your bags and we can be on our way."

"That's great, but we haven't eaten much. Can we stop somewhere and get a sandwich?"

"Sure, I need to call home and tell my mom we're leaving, too. There's a coffee shop across from the Forks Motel. We can go there."

It took Hank no time to load the luggage in his Chevy Monte Carlo and they walked a block to the coffee shop. While Angela and Lan ate, Hank called his mom in Three Rivers, a small community west of Forks.

His mother answered on the second ring. He listened intently and then hung up. *Damn!*

Pete and Ray gassed up at a Shell Station in West Olympia then picked up Highway 101 West and Highway 8 to the Aberdeen-Hoquiam area. Mostly they chatted about their days at the University, but Pete eventually brought up the subject of the investigation.

"How are your sessions with the shrink going?"

"So, so. He's still trying to get me to remember who did the rape at the house that night and who attacked me on our hike."

"You still don't remember anything I take it?"

"No. Only vague images so far, nothing definitive. We're going to have one more session next week."

"Do you still think it was Larry or Gordy or me?"

"I don't, but who could it have been? Although Sergeant Casper still does."

"Does what?"

"Think it's one of you three," Ray said, turning to look at Pete, who frowned.

"You like this Angela, huh?" Pete asked, obviously changing the subject.

"Yes."

"Well, good luck. Just let her know who's boss. Don't make the same mistake I did."

Ray was thinking about how to respond to Pete when he spotted the sign for Highway 101 North. "Here's where we turn."

Angela could tell that Hank's mood changed after they left the coffee shop. The cheery, talkative conversation that greeted them at the bus station was replaced by measured, short responses to Angela's questions and observations. *What's his problem?*

She wished she'd sat in back with Lan rather than on the front bench seat next to Hank. His body odor was overwhelming, and he definitely was preoccupied with something other than her banter and going way too fast for the curvy highway. She opened her window. As she did, Angela saw a road sign, which stated it was 5 miles to the Upper Hoh

Valley Road, 20 to Kalaloch and 57 to Amanda Park. *Not that much farther now*, she thought.

She wondered if Ranger Jerry Helspath still was at Kalaloch. She heard he'd recently been a member of a special search team and had gotten serious over one of the team members. Jerry had helped Angela out her first year in the Park.

"Would we have time to stop at the Ranger Station in Kalaloch?"

She turned toward Hank. *What! Was he checking me out?* Without seeming too obvious, she pulled her skirt down.

"I guess so," he said, quickly averting his eyes back to the road. *Damn,* he thought, *she's hot. Pushy, too*!

"I worked with one of the rangers there," Angela offered.

"Is that right. Say, I filled a thermos with coffee before we left Forks. It's on the back seat next to Lan. Going to be a long ride."

Looking over her shoulder, Angela saw that Lan had dozed off. She reached back and got the thermos. "You want a cup, too?"

"In a minute. I'm okay for now." He glanced sideways, watching Angela as she poured the coffee. Removing his right hand from the wheel, he reached in his jacket pocket.

"What's that?" she asked, as he pulled out his hand.

"Oh just a little bottle of some good smelling stuff."

Detective Casper had called Bill's number twice but gotten no answer. His bad luck continued when he tried to get someone at the Clallam County Sheriff's office. Everyone was either out to lunch or off for the day. His luck changed though when he got a call back from County Sheriff Ben Maxwell.

After some background information, he told Maxwell of his suspicions and asked him to stop Hank Mason from picking up the two girls and hold him for questioning.

Unfortunately, the good luck didn't last long. Maxwell called back to say that Hank wasn't at his home and when they'd called his mother in Three Rivers, she was less than cooperative. Then even more bad luck. When the deputy went to the bus station, all the inbound passengers had left. He did check, though, and found that Angela and Lan had been on the bus. The station manager did remember seeing a man helping two girls with their luggage. "One was Chinese, or something," he'd said.

Casper thought about this later and wondered why the deputy hadn't first gone to the bus station. *More bad luck!*

Ray and Pete pulled up in front of Bill's cabin in Amanda Park shortly after three. There was a note thumb tacked to the door. Bill wrote that he and Edie Cox had gone to the gift shop at the Kalaloch Lodge and should be back at four and to just go in, the door was unlocked.

They'd barely walked in when the phone rang. Ray answered. It was Sergeant Casper.

"Ray, that sounds like you?"

"Yeah, Pete and I just got here." He mouthed to Pete that it was Casper.

"I've been trying to get Bill all day," Casper said, almost screaming into the phone.

"He's up at Kalaloch. His note says he'll be back by four. What's the problem?"

"Are Angela and Lan there yet?" Casper asked.

"No, haven't seen them. They should be here any minute, though. You sound concerned, what's going on?"

"What's going on is that I think I know who your attacker was and who probably is the rapist and killer."

"You do?"

Pete was watching intently. He could sense from Ray's side of the conversation and his body language that something ominous had happened and tensed up when Ray turned and stared at him.

"What should we do?" Ray said to Casper.

Pete watched as Ray listened, occasionally saying yes and nodding his head. When he hung up, he stood still. Pete could see that the color had completely drained from his face.

"What is it, Ray? You look like you've seen the proverbial ghost."

"Casper's convinced he knows the identity of my attacker and the probable rapist."

"From your expression, I'd guess I'm off the short list."

"Yes, and Larry and Gordy too."

"So who is it?"

"He thinks it's Hank."

"Hank Mason, our Hank. Come on, there's got to be some mistake," Pete said.

"I hope so."

"So what are we supposed to do when Hank gets here? Act like nothing's wrong?"

Casper hung up the phone. He'd called the Sheriffs in Clallam and Jefferson County; he'd gotten hold of Ray, and phoned the Washington State Patrol. Hopefully, they could arrest Hank Mason before he discovered they were on to him. He told Ray to do nothing rash if Hank got there before they stopped him. He was also worried about the two women.

    The answer had been there all the time. He was sure he had a strong enough case to have Mason arrested on suspicion of attacking Ray. Proving Mason was the rapist was another thing. He told Ray what he'd heard on the tape from the pre-rush party that clearly made Hank their prime suspect.

    It was during the conversation in the beer line. Hank said, "crept out and cold cocked you." No other person in any of the recorded conversations had ever said anything about Ray being hit. Maybe he was jumping to conclusions, but Casper had a gut feeling about it, even though he couldn't figure out how Hank managed to have been at the campsite.

    That question aside, Casper kept returning to the taped conversation and the odd use of the word "crept." Then there was the fact that Mason had been present or in close proximity when at least three of the rapes had occurred. It was enough to convince him to call Sheriff Maxwell and the State Patrol.

    Casper was tempted to ask his boss whether he could drive to Amanda Park, even though it was out of his jurisdiction. He decided to wait and hope that the locals and the State Patrol would get the job done.

Ray heard the sound of a car and opened the cabin door just as Bill reached the top stair step.

    "I see you read the note. Sorry I'm a little late," Bill said. Entering, he extended his hand. "Welcome, I assume you're Pete?"

    Bill didn't look at all like what Pete had expected.

From the tales Ray had told, he anticipated seeing a heavily bearded, unkempt old man. Instead the man that shook his hand was clean-shaven, had a closely cropped haircut and other than his plaid wool shirt, looked more like a typical thirty-something from Seattle than a mountain man.

"Where are the girls?"

"Not here yet," said Ray.

Bill glanced at his newly purchased Bulova. "That's funny, I thought for sure they'd have beaten you guys."

"I know," said Ray. "I need to tell you what's going on."

Escape to the Hoh

The Hoh River meanders through one of the world's most renowned rain forests. Every year thousands of visitors journey to Washington's Olympic Peninsula to visit the Hoh Rain Forest and see the breathtaking beauty of its incredible assembly of plant life.

The Upper Hoh River road provides access to the Park's Visitor Center, the many trails that border the river and to the mountains beyond.

When Hank Mason told Ray that he had hiked both in the Copper Creek/Tull Canyon area and in the Hoh Valley, it was an understatement. He had spent countless days discovering the secrets of Tull Canyon and had taken several recent excursions in the Hoh area, exploring the lush forest and climbing the steep cliffs of Mount Tom, Mount Carrie and Mount Olympus. The summer before he started at the University, he discovered a deserted miner's cabin near Falls Creek.

Hal Burton

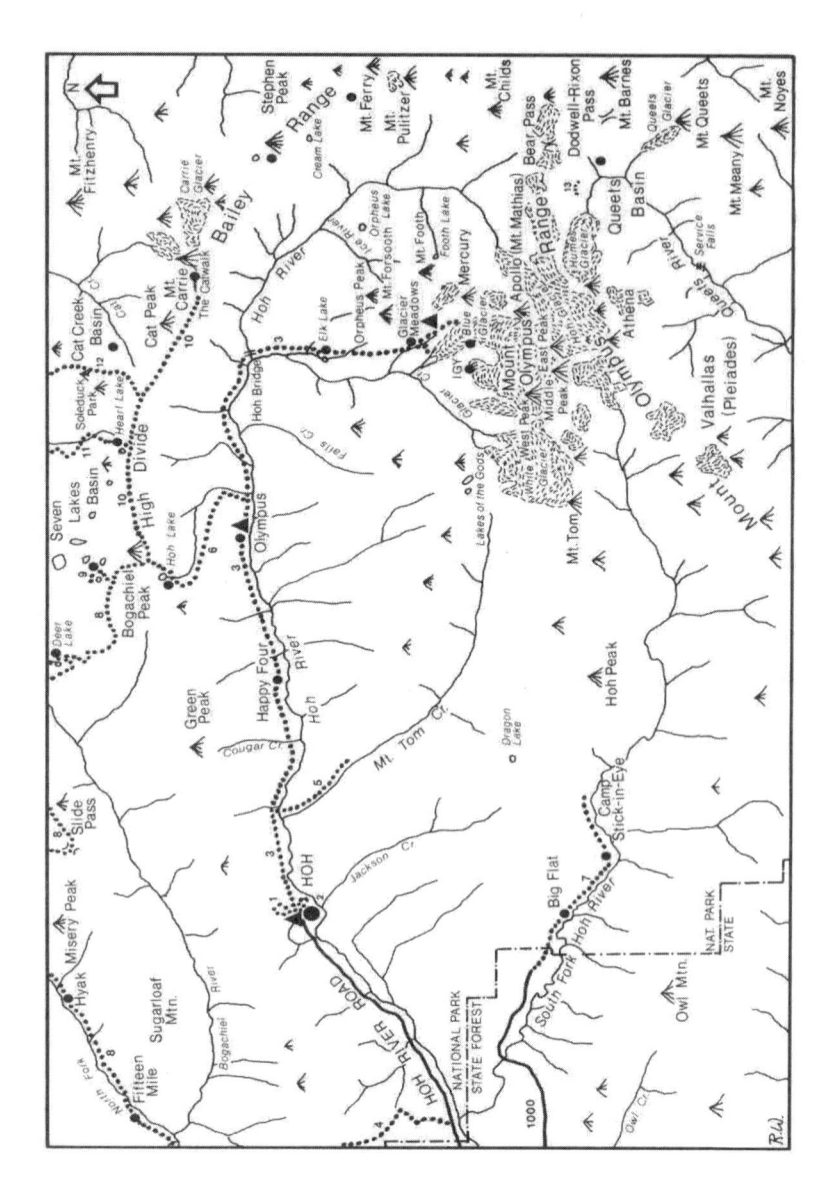

The Hoh Trial

Convinced that the authorities were on to him, it was to this haven that he now retreated. The phone call to his mom's house from the sheriff's office was proof enough. He looked across at Angela, now fast asleep just like Lan. *This might be fun, after all*, he thought, his cravings on the rise.

He slowed for the left turn onto Upper Hoh River road.

Angela stirred next to him. The sleeping pills he put in the coffee should be enough to keep both of the women quiet for at least another hour. The rope he got out of the trunk when he stopped at the trailhead to Peak 6, would be put to use later. For now, he was content to let them both snooze away.

When Hank and the women weren't at Bill's cabin in Amanda Park by six o'clock, Ray was convinced that something was wrong. Ray called the number he had for Hank, but got no answer. Next he called Sergeant Casper in Seattle.

Casper was still at work. He told Ray that both the Clallam and Jefferson County Sheriff's offices and the State Patrol were looking for Hank. They knew at this point that Hank had met the women at the bus station.

"Either they've had car problems or Hank got wind of our warrant and took off. Unfortunately, if the latter is true, we have to assume he's got Angela and Lan Thi with him," Casper said.

Ray listened in silence, but Bill could tell from his expression that it wasn't good news. Ray hung up the phone.

"I guess all we can do is just wait" he said, looking at Bill and shaking his head. "Hank's probably just had car problems," Ray suggested, not wanting to accept the other alternative.

"Casper doesn't really believe that, does he?" Bill said.

"No, not really."

"Besides," Bill suggested, "if the car broke down, the State Patrol would have seen them."

Ray turned to Pete. "Pete, there's no reason for you to stick around. Thanks for the ride, and it sure looks like I owe Larry and Gordy a big apology."

"What, how about me!" Pete said

"I never really thought it was you. I wouldn't have accepted the ride if I had, but if it makes you feel better," Ray bowed low. " I apologize."

Pete smiled. "Apology accepted, but if it's all right with you, I'll stick around. Maybe I can help."

"Sure, but I don't really know what we can do, except wait."

The morning brought only more frustration. Casper had called just before eleven the night before to let them know that they still had not located Hank. Then after a sleepless night, they were awakened early by calls from both Jefferson and Clallam County Sheriffs telling them essentially the same thing, no sighting of Hank or his car.

Ray, Bill and Pete would recall later that the next call they received brought both good and bad news. They had located Hank's car parked at the Hoh Rain Forest Visitor's Center. A Park Ranger who at first was not suspicious, assuming it belonged to a hiker, spotted the car. However, when he opened the station office he found the All-Points Bulletin from the State Patrol and checking the license, realized it was the Monte Carlo for which they were looking. How long the car had been there, he didn't know, but it wasn't there when he went off shift at 4 P.M. the day before.

When the State Patrol searched inside the car they found little to substantiate that the two women had been there, but when they pried open the trunk they found a knapsack and a cosmetic bag. A name card in a leather holder of the knapsack identified the owner as Angela Rhodes. The cosmetic bag contained a pain prescription for Lan Thi. There was also a note addressed to, "Ray and his helpers."

You are obviously on my trail if you've found this note. I suggest you not try to follow me. My two female companions I find quite delectable – you know, Angela and Lan. Oh my, what sweet things they are and ripe for the picking. I will let them go eventually – ha ha. Call off your dogs! Your brother in the bind. Hank

Ray shuddered as the note was read to him and said out loud, "He's gone crazy."

Bill and Pete reacted with equal shock as Ray told what the State Trooper had related. Ray finished by telling them that both county sheriffs were en route to the Hoh Visitor's Center to help with the search.

"That's where we're going too," said Bill, very emphatically. "We know that area about as well as anyone. Pete, it's up to you, if you want to tag along."

"Well, as my grandfather used to say, "In for a penny, in for a pound."

"All right. Ray you start getting our gear together while I ask Edie if we can borrow her jeep. By the way, your pack and bow and arrows are in the cabinet on the back porch."

"Shall we let the sheriff know we're coming?"

Bill nodded. "Yeah, give him a call."

The area around Hank's Monte Carlo and the Hoh River trailhead was cordoned off with yellow tape. Three State Patrol cars and two County Sheriff's vehicles were parked around the perimeter. More tape was strung between two sawhorses, several hundred yards down the road, where a Park Ranger was telling drivers to turn around.

The ranger had obviously been told to expect them. As soon as they identified themselves, they were waved through after being told to report to Sheriff Wilcox of Jefferson County.

A deputy told Bill that Sheriff Wilcox was inside the Visitor's Center, but called over Sheriff Maxwell from Clallam County. After brief introductions, Maxwell escorted them to the Center, which had been set up as the command post. As they walked he brought them up to date.

Two search teams were combing the area looking for any clues to where Hank had gone. One of these teams had been as far as the junction to the Mount Tom Creek Trail, about three miles up the Hoh River Trail from the Visitor's Center. The second team was searching along the two Nature Trails. A third team was continuing to go over Hank's car and exploring the perimeter around the Visitor's Center.

As Bill, Ray and Pete entered the Center, Wilcox and his deputy were discussing whether to have the first team of four men continue east on the Hoh River Trail or to split up at Tom Creek. So far they reported finding nothing out of the ordinary.

Bill didn't wait for introductions, but stepped forward of Maxwell and walked up to Wilcox. "Let Ray and I join your team. That will give you two more men. I know the area quite well and Ray does too."

Wilcox turned to face Bill. "Mr. O'Hara, and I assume this is Ray Wellsford and Pete Fairchild."

"Sorry, Dick," said Maxwell.

"That's okay, Ben, in fact, my deputy and I were just

discussing the possibility. We can use the help and from what I've heard, Mr. O'Hara does know the Park about as well as anybody."

"We've got a lot at stake too, remember," said Ray.

"Yes, I quite understand. So, let me tell you what we know," Wilcox said. "I figure we've still got several hours before it starts getting dark."

Most of what Sheriff Wilcox related, they already were familiar with. The car had been definitely identified as Hank's and they knew it had been left in the parking lot sometime after four PM the previous day. Other than the knapsack and the cosmetic bag, no traces of Angela and Lan Thi had been found either in the car or in the area that had been searched.

"May I see the note from Hank?" Ray asked.

"Sure." Wilcox handed a single sheet of paper to Ray.

Ray read it to himself and then, he raised it to his nose. "What's that smell?"

"Musk cologne or after-shave lotion," Maxwell answered.

Pete, who hadn't said anything up to this point reached out for the sheet of paper. "Let me see," he said, taking a big sniff. "Yup, that smells like Hank's favorite."

"You never mentioned that before, Pete," Ray said plaintively, realizing the implications.

Hide and Seek

Bill and Ray were making good time thanks to a level, carpet-like trail and figured they'd meet the search team at Tom Creek in another fifteen minutes. Sheriff Wilcox had radioed ahead and told the team to wait. Pete reluctantly stayed at the Command Center.

"Under different circumstances, I'd be happy to be back on the trail with you, Ray."

"I know, but I can tell already that I'm out of shape."

"Me too."

"Do you think Hank expects to be followed?"

"Oh, I think so for sure. His note to you was just a tease. He expects it. I think for him, it's part of his game," Bill said.

Ray almost plowed into Bill when he stopped suddenly. "Did you notice that deep scrape across the path, back a ways?"

"No."

Bill knelt down. "The one here," he said, pointing to a deep furrow just at the trail's edge, "looked just like this."

Ray shook his head. "Sorry, I don't remember seeing it."

"You've forgotten what I taught you. A good tracker always has his eyes on the trail."

"That mark could have been left by anyone."

"I know," said Bill, but — if we had time I'd go back and take a look see at the other one I saw. Okay, probably just hoping for something. Lan Thi was always clever at marking our trails in Viet Nam and she often used her shoe heel. Let's go!"

The trail narrowed and rocks took the place of the soft under-footing of rotting vegetation. Had there been any more "marks," they would have been hard to see. Up ahead, Bill spotted the search team. "Looks like we're here."

Before leaving the Center, Bill had suggested to Sheriff Wilcox that three of the advance team search the trail that follows Tom Creek and then Cougar Creek, before heading back for the night. He and Ray, plus one of the team, would continue on to Happy Four Shelter, another three miles, search that area and stay there for the night. Beyond Happy Four, there were so many possible directions one could go that the task seemed overwhelming.

Joined by Sheriff's Deputy Kyle Peterson, Ray and Bill set off for Happy Four Shelter. Darkness would soon be upon them, yet Bill's pace still allowed them ample opportunity to scan the glades of alders on either side of their trail.

"What are we looking for, exactly?" asked Peterson. "He could be anywhere."

"I know," said Bill, "but, we really don't have much choice and for me, it's better than sitting around waiting."

"Bill," Ray called, look here!" he said, pointing to the edge of the trail.

"Damn, I missed that. Good eyes Ray."

"What is it?" said Peterson.

What Ray had spotted, was another of the marks in the trail that they had seen before. It was about six to eight inches long, running at right angles to the trail path.

"We saw two similar signs back a mile or so. Could be a fluke, maybe not. Let's keep going."

Hank was in the lead, followed single file by Angela and Lan. Each of the women's hands was tightly bound and they were tethered together at their waists. He had alternated between leading and following, occasionally stopping to check on the bindings. Keeping two women under wraps and maintaining any kind of pace had been difficult, but he guessed he could still make it to the cabin by nightfall. He had hit Lan once. She limped and was constantly dragging her feet, slowing their progress. He'd been tempted to retie them, putting Lan in front, but didn't want to stop. Angela seemed to still be under the influence of the pills and her staggering further hampered setting any faster speed.

He originally planned on staying in the cabin on Glacier Creek for several days, enjoying his company and then heading to his final destination and escape. Now he realized that taking both women the distance would not be possible. One he would have to leave at the cabin and also he would only stay one night. *No sense underestimating the cops*, he thought. The choice was easy. Lan would not continue on.

The cabin had been neglected for so many years that from a distance it seemed to be part of the color pallet of giant ferns and moss-shrouded trees.

Hank had added a few amenities to the inside, but left the outside untouched. He slid the lock bolt to the side and pulled the women inside, pushing them down on the floor. Next he retrieved a Coleman lantern from a cabinet.

"Starting to get dark," he said, lighting the lantern. "I'll bet you're getting hungry, too."

The two women didn't react.

"Maybe you need to go potty," he said with a chuckle.

Angela, now more alert, responded. "Yes. That would be appreciated."

"I'll go uncover the pit and get some water. You just rest easy and don't do anything stupid, I'll be just a minute."

It was the first chance they'd had to talk. "Where are we?" asked Lan.

"A couple miles off the main Hoh River Trail. I think that creek we crossed was Falls Creek. Not real sure though, I've been out of it until the last hour or so."

Lan heard Hank returning and spoke quickly. "I've been marking the trail . . ." Hank was back.

"Come on, before it's too dark." He grabbed Angela's rope end and led them outside to the pit toilet.

"It's out in the open," said Angela.

"Not my problem. I won't peek, ha ha."

Hank wasn't prepared to feed himself for several days, let alone two other mouths. Leaving Lan would help. He ate some of the trail mix he'd put in the cabinet on his last trip and offered Lan and Angela a handful.

"That will have to do. Here's some water," he said, handing them one of the two canteens.

As the women ate he contemplated what to do with Lan. She didn't excite him like Angela did and within the small confines of the one room cabin he couldn't have some fun with Lan without Angela watching. That idea, however, held some appeal, but he discarded it. She was just too docile for his tastes, no fight in her and it was fight he liked.

Should he just tie her up and leave her in the morning, or kill her? If he left her tied up, chances are someone would find her before she died. She wouldn't know where he was heading. Finally, he decided to see how it went that night and make his decision in the morning.

He threw them one of the two blankets he had and tethered their rope to an overhead beam. "Better get some sleep."

Hank didn't sleep well, as he constantly worried about the women trying something. He wished he'd had more of the pills. Before it was even light, he was putting what provisions he had in his backpack and rolling up the blanket. He ate some more of the trail mix before leaving the cabin to fill the canteens. The women had not stirred.

As soon as the door closed, Angela moved slightly away from Lan. "You awake?" she whispered.

"Yes, for some time."

"Looks like we're going. We need some kind of plan."

Before they could continue, Hank returned. "Well, looks like you're up from your beauty sleep," he said sarcastically.

Hank set the canteens down and before they realized what was going on, he cut the tether between them and pulled Lan away from Angela. The rope holding Angela was still attached to the overhead beam.

"Come on little Miss Saigon, we're going for a walk."

Bill and Ray found two more of the distinctive marks on the trail to Happy Four Shelter. There may have been more, but as the sunlight faded, they were lucky just to stay on the trail. Peterson radioed in that they were calling it quits for the day. Going on the assumption that the "marks" were left by one of the women, in the morning they would continue east, towards Mt. Olympus. Sheriff Wilcox reported that they had found no further evidence of Hank or the women along the main trail. The other team would backtrack and search along the south fork of the Hoh River, as far as Big Flat.

They had the pick of campsites at Happy Four. Bill hoped that someone would be camping there and perhaps would have seen Hank and the women. After a hastily prepared meal, they pitched their tent and crawled into their sleeping bags. It was just after seven PM.

Bill was up at dawn and had the fire going. He knew it was going to be a crucial day. If they couldn't find any trace of Hank and the women before they got to the junction of the trail to Hoh Lake, they'd have to split up or stay together and search first one direction, then backtrack and search the other. It would be a time-consuming task. He was beginning to have doubts about finding their quarry.

The trail descended as they left camp and in about two miles, crossed the river at Eight-Mile Slough. Bill hadn't been in this area since the Hoh Lake fire in 1978. He was amazed how vegetation was growing back, as the fire had killed most of the trees and destroyed all the ground cover. Now the scarred terrain was in sharp contrast to the new greenery.

It was when they recrossed the slough and entered the spur blackened by the fire that Ray spotted another of the telltale signs at the trail's edge.

"Looks like we're still on track if these marks are what we think they are," said Bill.

"I should radio the others," Peterson said. " I hope I'm still in range."

"Yes, go ahead. Tell them we're going on to the Olympus Station and also find out if they've found anything."

Kyle Peterson was able to make contact and learned the other teams, not finding any traces of Hank and the women, had ceased searching. It was now up to them.

The Olympus Ranger Station was unmanned due to federal budget cuts, and was falling on disrepair. Still, it did have potable water and a pit toilet, so they took a break.

"This is it, you know," said Bill. "In less than a mile, the trail splits and unless we find one of those marks right away, we're literally screwed." Bill handed the map to Ray.

"What should we do?"

"Ray, I'm just not sure. My guess is to follow the main trail as far as Glacier Creek and see what we come across."

"What then?" Peterson asked.

"Then we either go ahead or backtrack and take the Hoh Lake Trail." Bill turned to Ray. "What we really need are some of those voices you once heard to tell us which way to go."

While Bill, Ray and Deputy Peterson rested at the abandoned Olympus Ranger Station, several miles north Hank, with Angela in tow, was on the Hoh Lake Trail, heading toward Bogachiel Peak and the Soleduck River.

"Come on, you're slowing us down," Hank said, pulling on the rope.

"That hurts, you bastard."

"Ah, that's what I like. You're back to your feisty self. Tonight should be fun."

Several times she'd asked and each time he'd refused to tell her what had become of Lan. All he would say and always with a grin, was that she was communing with nature. Angela feared the worst and had resisted leaving the cabin that morning, but Hank had slapped her around and yanked her out the door, leading her back down the trail and north over the fire-devastated landscape approaching Hoh Lake.

Angela couldn't believe that they hadn't met someone along the trail. Hank had warned her not to talk if they did, but why wouldn't anyone think it odd that they were roped together on an easily walked trail?

A Faint Voice

Since regaining consciousness, Lan struggled to remove the gag, but with her hands still tightly bound and tied behind her to the trunk, she'd made little progress. However, by rubbing her face against the tree, she had loosened her blindfold enough to see the light.

She was convinced Hank was going to rape her when he had forced her to remove her clothes. Instead, he silently watched, then after throwing most of her clothes over the bank behind the pit toilet, he'd lashed her to a nearby tree. She was sure he was going to kill her, but he only slapped her hard across her breasts and face, used her shirt to fashion a blindfold and gag and walked away. Hank hadn't said much, but as he departed he told her that she would be a good meal for a hungry bear and added, "Too bad you'll miss our trip to the wild blue yonder, but there's only room for two."

She knew she was tied to one of the cluster of fir trees on the bank below the pit toilet, in full view of anyone on the west side, but hidden from someone on the trail or in the cabin.

Lan's face was getting raw, but twisting around, she resumed rubbing her face up and down against the bark of the tree, slowly slackening the gag.

She tried shouting, but the sound was still muffled, sounding more like someone grunting. By now she figured the right side of her face was bleeding for it certainly hurt. She shifted and turned her left side to the task, first working on the blindfold, then the gag. How long she kept at it she wasn't sure, but now her whole body ached and a cool breeze added to her misery as it played across her nakedness. *Time for a rest*, she thought.

Half asleep, she wasn't sure whether it was her imagination or not when she heard voices. No, she was sure. She did hear voices, coming from behind her. She had to yell.

Ray hadn't seen any more of the marks since passing the junction with the Hoh Lake Trail, but as planned, the three men had continued on to Glacier Creek. They crossed over Lake Creek and skirted around a meadow where Bill said there used to be a cabin similar to an old one further on near Falls Creek.

"When we get to Glacier Creek I'll radio in," said Kyle.

"Okay," Bill answered. "Let's stop at Falls Creek for a minute, I'm getting low on water."

"Do you have any more of the iodine pills?" Ray asked.

"Just one. Next time we'll have to boil some water unless you have some."

"No, I don't."

"There's the bridge over the creek just ahead," Bill said, pointing. He turned to Kyle, "Why don't you see if you can make contact while we stop here, it's only a mile to Glacier anyway?"

Bill took off his pack and knelt to fill his canteen.

"Did you hear that, Ray asked?"

"You mean the static?"

"No! Kyle, hold on for a minute."

"I don't hear anything but the sound of the creek." Then, he did. "Yes! Sounds like it's coming from up there," Bill said, indicating a stand of fir trees on the hillside above them.

"There, again, come on let's take a look."

"The old cabin I discovered two years ago is up there," said Bill, now running ahead of the other two.

Lan heard them approaching and thought sure she recognized Bill's voice. She pursed her lips enough to stretch the cloth and yelled with all her might.

"Over here. I'm behind the trees!"

Bill knew that voice. "Lan, Lan, I'm coming."

As he reached the crest of the hill he spotted her and quickly stopped and turned, holding out his arms. "I'll get her, you two search the cabin." Puzzled why Bill stopped them so quickly, Ray and Kyle nevertheless changed direction and headed for the cabin.

Removing his coat, Bill hurriedly continued.

"Oh my God, Lan. Here." He wrapped his coat around her and swiftly cut the ropes and removed the gag and blindfold and took her into his arms. Pulling back slightly, he saw her badly scraped face and swore to himself that if he caught Hank, he would make sure he had a painful and slow death.

"Come on, let's get you cleaned up."
"He threw my clothes down that bank."
Bill lowered Lan down to the ground. "Yes, I see them. Wait a minute."
Just then Ray hollered up. "How is she?"
"Cold, scared and bloodied, otherwise not too bad. I'm going to help her clean up and then we'll be down. Any sign of Angela or Hank?"
"No. They were here for sure, though." said Ray.
Bill turned his attention back to Lan, who by now had put her clothes on. She wore Bill's coat. He soaked his handkerchief in water and dabbed at her face.
"Ouch. Here, let me do it." Through the tears and scrapes a smile took form. "This isn't the way I imagined meeting you again."
"I don't care. You're beautiful to me." Then hesitantly, "Did he …ah … hurt you? I mean …"
"Did he rape me, no. I fully expected that when he made me undress, but he just watched, ... then he ..." She hesitated. "Then he hit me in the chest and slapped me."
He pulled her close again and for a moment neither said anything.
"Did you hear him leave with Angela?"
"No. Oh, I just remembered something odd he said."
"About Angela?"
"In a way. He said there was only room for two in the wild blue yonder, or something like that."
"That is weird." It didn't register as anything in particular. *A comment from someone who is definitely wacky*, he thought. "If you're okay, let's go down and see what Ray and Deputy Peterson are up to."
As they started walking, Lan staggered and almost collapsed. "I think you're worse off than you'll admit," Bill said. "We need to get you to a doctor."

"What about Angela?"

"We'll see about that, but first let's get you taken care of," Bill said, as he put his arm tightly around her and led her down the hill to the cabin.

She looked up at him. "Oh Bill, I'd almost given up."

Convinced that Lan Thi needed medical attention and not having any clues to where Hank had taken Angela, they decided to return to the Hoh Ranger Station. From what Bill had learned from Lan, he figured Hank had a couple hours' lead and it was frustrating not to keep on his trail.

Ray, especially, was sure that he could catch them if Hank stayed on the main trails. The problem was, which one. He doubted they'd continued on toward Glacier Meadows and the trail to Mt. Olympus and that meant they had to have backtracked and taken the trail to Hoh Lake. However, once on the Hoh Lake Trail, Hank had several routes he could take. That even assumed he was on the trail. He could be hiding in any one of many remote valleys or in a cave like the one he and Bill had shared.

"Why don't you and Kyle take Lan back and I'll take the Hoh Lake Trail," he suggested to Bill.

"No, I think we need to stick together. There's no point in you taking off by yourself if you don't know where he went. Besides, we had Lan's trail marks to help us before."

He squeezed Lan's hand. "I assume that was you who left the trail marks for us?"

"Yes. You see, I didn't forget the tricks we used in my homeland."

"Did Angela know you were doing it?" Ray asked.

"No, we had very little opportunity to talk, Lan said quietly.

Bill knew Ray well enough to tell that he was frustrated and not in agreement. *Maybe Ray <u>should</u> take the Hoh Lake Trail while they took Lan to the ranger station*, he thought.

Ray broke the awkward silence. "Okay, let's go. I'll decide when we get to the junction with the lake trail. I just have a gut feeling he's going to head that way."

As they hiked, Lan told them more of what she remembered of their ordeal and told Ray how sorry she was that she couldn't help more concerning Angela.

"He is a bad man and crazy, too, I think."

"That's for sure," said Ray, "crazier than a loon."

Bill chimed in. "Yeah, he even told Lan there was no room for her in the wild blue yonder. Nuttier than the proverbial fruitcake that frat brother of yours."

"What did he say?" Ray said. Something was tickling his memory. "The wild blue yonder?"

"Yes, the blue yonder, or wild blue yonder. Something like that."

Deputy Peterson plowed into Ray when he stopped suddenly, almost knocking Ray over. "What the …"

"Sorry Kyle. Bill hold up!" Ray called.

"What is it?"

"I think I know where Hank is heading."

Tubal Cain

In 1899 copper and manganese ore were discovered near Tull Canyon on the northeast side of the Olympic Mountains. By 1900 the small town of Tull City prospered near the mine that was aptly named Tubal Cain after the Old Testament book of Genesis metal forger, Tubal-Cain. Many of the miners were Chinese immigrants that had arrived at the then flourishing coastal town of Port Townsend. Diminishing high-grade ore, skyrocketing maintenance costs, unbearable winter conditions and spring floods finally closed the mine in 1912.

Within a few years the damp forest reclaimed most of Tubal Cain Camp. What didn't rot or burn soon turned to rust and blended into the landscape. A shaft at the top of a gigantic tailings' pile marks the entrance to the deserted mine that tunnels over 2800 feet into the earth.

Adjacent Tull Canyon is also the site of the wreckage of a search-and-rescue B-17, which crashed during a January 1952 snowstorm. Most of the debris is strewn over the basin that lies below the crash site, a mountain ridge, about 2000 feet above.

Voices from the Mountain

Bill didn't believe what he heard. "You've got to be kidding!"

"No, I'm not and when we get to the junction, I'm heading that way, with or without you."

"But that's miles away. He'd have to take the High Divide, then Appleton Pass and then somehow connect with Hurricane Ridge and he'd still have miles to go to reach the Dungeness. No, I just don't buy it. Besides, we assume he's got Angela with him and as far as we know he has no provisions or gear for a hike like that."

They were nearing the junction with the Hoh Lake Trail, which Ray was convinced, was the route taken by Hank. Ray remembered Hank telling him about his hikes in Tull Canyon, and the references to "wild blue yonder" could only refer to the site of the B-17 crash. Bill was right about one thing, though, getting there alone would be a huge undertaking and with Angela in tow, an almost impossible task. Ray was certain that Hank was just crazy enough to try it.

"Why would he go there, of all places?" Bill asked Ray.

It was Peterson that came up with one plausible answer. "He'd be close to several roads that lead to Highway 101 and from there he could get to Sequim or Quilcene."

"Maybe," said Ray. "Anyway, here's where I leave you."

"Wait!" Bill turned to Peterson. "Kyle, maybe you should go with Ray. I can get Lan back okay."

"Bill, you should go," Lan interjected.

"No. I lost you once, not again."

"I'll go." Peterson looked questioningly. "Ray?"

"That's fine with me and the wireless will come in handy. Thanks, it may be a wild goose chase, but I don't think so."

So it was settled. Bill and Lan headed down the trail to the Hoh Station and Ray and Kyle turned northeast towards Hoh

Lake and the High Divide. Before departing, Bill gave all his provisions, including his full quill of arrows, to Ray.

"Hope you don't have to use these. Remember everything I taught you and be careful, desperate people do desperate things."

"Thanks, you be careful too and Lan, I'm glad you're okay."

She smiled. "Yes, now go find Angela."

Ted and Linda Spears got the tackle box and poles and left their campsite just after dawn. That's when Ted said the trout fishing would be the best. He'd found a nice spot where Hoh Creek flowed into the lake. The hike up the steep, switchbacking trail the day before had sapped their energy, but now, excited about the prospects of landing some Rainbow Trout on Ted's handmade flies, they eagerly set out.

By nine they had their limit and headed back to camp to, as Ted said, "clean these babies up for a nice meal." Their reaction to the sight that greeted them was at first, one of total surprise and amazement, and then anger set in. Save for a few scattered pieces of clothing and two dirty pie tins, everything else was gone. Their tent, sleeping bags, food, backpacks and utensils were nowhere to be seen. Initially, Ted thought maybe a bear had invaded their camp, but there was no evidence of that and besides, things weren't destroyed, they were gone. Some two-legged animals had sneaked into the camp while they were fishing.

Having little choice, they gathered what few things remained and headed back to where they left their car at the Hoh Station.

Just before reaching the main Hoh Trail, they encountered Ray and Kyle Peterson. Seeing Kyle's badge they told their sad story. After only a few sentences into Ted Spears' tale, Ray knew the identity of the culprit.

"How long ago would you say your stuff was taken?" Ray asked.

"Let's see. We left camp around six and got back about nine-thirty, so some time in-between there."

Kyle could almost see Ray's "wheels' turning." He too did a quick calculation after looking at his watch. It was now just after eleven. Hiking up the steep grade to Hoh Lake would take he and Ray a couple of hours, so worst case scenario, Hank had about a six-hour head start.

Kyle made two unsuccessful attempts to contact Sheriff Wilcox, but not wanting to take any more time, he told the Spears to report all that had happened when they reached the Hoh Ranger Station. He would try radioing later when they got up higher for he needed to report that they had fairly conclusive evidence that Hank was heading north towards the Seven Lakes Basin. He was going to suggest that they start searching the area with helicopters when the cloud cover lifted.

The six plus miles up to Hoh Lake were a real grind and it was nearing three o'clock when they reached the junction with Bogachiel Peak Trail and High Divide. Deputy Peterson had talked to Sheriff Wilcox and learned that Bill and Lan had made it back safely, as had the Spears. Reviewing all the possibilities with the Park Rangers, the consensus was that it would take a minimum of two days to reach the Dungeness region. Bill got on the line and tried once again to convince Ray to turn back.

"If you're positive he's going to Tull Canyon, it would be quicker for you to come back here and drive around east of Sequim and hike in from there," he said.

"What if he leaves Angela along the way, like he did Lan?" Ray countered.

Bill couldn't argue with that logic.

"Okay, you go ahead. They're going to use the helicopters tomorrow and now that Lan's safe, I'm going to drive around and hike in to Tull Canyon. I sure hope you're right about this."

Hank pitched the tent in a dense stand of Douglas fir and western hemlock. He could have gone on to the Upper Soleduck camp but was afraid there might be campers. He'd been lucky today. They'd seen no one on the trail since leaving Hoh Lake. Angela had been warned several times of what would happen if she gave anything away and in general, she had been quite docile. She currently was tied to one of the small hemlocks, a gag stuffed in her mouth. Tonight he would have her all to himself. First things first. He was hungry and it looked like it might rain. Actually it was cold enough to snow, especially at their altitude.

It also occurred to him that someone, the sheriff, maybe Ray and his pal Bill, were close behind and could catch up if he stayed too long. He'd even thought of hiking until dark, but the next several miles of trail were treacherous enough in daylight. Soon it would be dark and if he didn't build a fire, he wouldn't be spotted and he finally reasoned that anyone following him would have to stop for the night, too.

Hank untied Angela and led her to the tent.

"Stay in here and be quiet." He pulled the tent flap closed, sat down on a nearby tree stump and took inventory of the pilfered cache of food and gear from Lake Hoh. He concluded that with what he already had, it should be enough to get him to Tull Canyon and Tubal Cain. Hank set aside two energy bars and two oranges and opening the tent flap, placed everything in the tent.

"Here's dinner," he said, tossing a bar and an orange to Angela. "Oh, I guess you can't eat with that gag, can you," giggling at his not-so-funny joke. "I'll take it off, but any loud noise and it goes right back on."

Angela nodded and unwrapped the bar. She was starved and cold, very cold. It wasn't cold or hunger, though that was most on her mind. It was the dread of the night ahead with Hank.

All day she'd been thinking of different plans on how to escape. She thought she had a chance when Hank was hurrying to take down the tent, but he seemed to read her mind and stopped long enough to tie her to a nearby log. Then, just a few minutes ago when he left the tent, she thought maybe she could tear the rear of the tent and crawl out, but she heard him right outside the tent and knew he would hear her.

Hank broke into her musings with an uncannily perceptive observation. "Don't even think of it! I'm not that stupid." He handed her a canteen. "Don't dare try anything or I'll push you off one of these cliffs."

"Just like you did to Ray?"

He didn't respond.

She took the offered water and glared at him, but said nothing more.

"C'mon it's time for a goodnight pee." He rose and taking hold of the rope around her waist, pulled her out of the tent.

A few feet beyond the tent he stopped. "Here, this is a good spot." Without releasing the end of the rope, he unzipped his pants, pulled out his penis and started peeing. Angela looked away.

"You'd better squat while you have the chance. Oh, oh, look, this baby's starting to get excited!" He yanked her closer. "Don't worry, your time will come. I'm saving you for later."

Angela's bladder was full to overflowing and she knew she'd never make it through the night, so pulling as far away as possible, she relieved herself. Out of the corner of her eye she saw Hank stroking himself.

When Bill and Lan arrived at the Hoh Ranger Station, one of the welcoming group was SPD Sergeant Dave Casper. Not willing to just sit and wait in Seattle, he had arrived that very morning. The State Patrol brought a nurse from Forks and she whisked Lan away into the ladies restroom.

Sheriff's Wilcox and Maxwell, two State Troopers, Bill and Pete thrashed out what to do next. Wilcox led the discussion and gave them some background information he'd uncovered on Hank, his mother and his biological father. That information alone convinced them, especially Bill, that most of the search team should head for Tull Canyon. A few others would go to the Soleduck Ranger Station just in case Hank outsmarted them and headed that way. When the weather cleared, the helicopters would start their search.

Bill remembered Ray mentioning once that Hank's stepfather was in prison, but he guessed that Ray didn't know the rest of the story.

The Best Laid Plans

Hank miscalculated and by midday he had realized it would take another day, maybe two, to reach his destination. Part of the problem was the damned helicopters, he had told himself. It seemed like every time he hiked in the open, he heard the approaching choppers and had to run for cover, pulling Angela along. Then instead of using the road going toward Lake Mills he had to tramp through the brush alongside for fear drivers headed to the Boulder Creek Campground would spot them.

    The sight of the Dungeness River on the morning of the third day lifted his spirits for he knew it would only be a few more hours. More than once he'd considered "taking her" and getting rid of Angela, but his overwhelming desire to show his sexual prowess to his father had prevailed. He also knew that if they did catch up to him, Angela would be an invaluable bargaining chip.

    She'd been cooperative the past day and a half, not even complaining as he had quickened his pace to stay ahead of his pursuers. He was sure they were behind him somewhere, but now, safely in the territory he'd explored in detail from age twelve and under the protective shield of thick clouds, he was on a high. He would soon be there.

Hank was right about being pursued, but Ray and Kyle were not as close as they had hoped to be. Once they left the Hurricane Ridge area, the terrain had been unfamiliar to Ray and at one juncture, he was convinced he was lost. Fortunately one of the search helicopters spotted them and gave him the heading to the Forest Service road that took them to the trailhead of Cameron Creek Trail and the route west towards the Dungeness River Valley. The helicopter also dropped them some food. It was a good thing it had been yesterday, because today the clouds had rolled in. The hiking pace was also taking its toll on Deputy Peterson. Where Ray was used to the regimen of backpacking in the high country, Kyle was not.

Bill and the search team from the Hoh Station weren't fairing any better at getting east of Sequim and the road to the trailhead. A rockslide on US Hwy 101, just west of the Lake Crescent Lodge had them blocked for five hours. They would be lucky to get on the trail before the next morning.

The only good thing about the delay, as far as Bill was concerned, was that he and Lan had time together. The nurse had given her a good bill of health and that said, there was no way Lan wasn't going with them.

"Are you sure you're feeling okay?" he said as he lowered himself down next to her. They sat on one of the several logs in the clearing where they'd pulled off.

"Yes! What's that American expression – "All right all ready!"

"Sorry."

"Just kidding, as you say. How much longer do you think it will be before the rockslide is cleared?" Lan asked, reaching out to take his hand.

"I'd guess at least an hour." He squeezed her hand and pulled her close. "We've got a lot of time to make up, though, so if it wasn't for our need to find this killer before he hurts Angela, I wouldn't mind the delay. I missed you so."

She looked up at him. "I hope we're in time."

Time was something that Hank wasn't worrying about any more.

"We're here," he announced proudly.

Angela wasn't really sure exactly where "here" was. She'd seen a Forest Service sign that said, "Copper Creek," a mile or so back and from what she remembered, they must be near Buckhorn Lake and Tull Canyon.

"Where?"

"At the site of Tubal Cain Camp. C'mon, we're going up there," he said, pointing above a huge hill of loose rock behind them. Above the rocks, a shear granite-like precipice rose at least five-hundred feet. "That's the pile of tailings from the mine. The entrance is on top, below that overhang. You'll see."

Hank led her up the barely perceptible trail that skirted the left side of the pile of tailings. The rock was loose and the grade steep. More than once, Angela slipped, but Hank seemed to have the legs of a mountain goat and dug in, keeping her from falling while continuing to pull her upward.

When they reached the top on the tailings pile, the mine entrance came into sight. The front edge of the tailings' pile was only twenty feet from the entrance, which appeared to be about seven feet high by five feet wide, rectangular in shape. A steady flow of water, about two inches in depth, flowed out of the opening and trickled down the steep hill to their left.

Angela held back. "We're going in there?"

"Yes."

He removed Linda Spears' purloined backpack from Angela and pushed her in the direction of the mine opening. *It was now or never*, she thought. She'd been working at loosening the knot in the rope around her waist for several hours and it felt like one quick pull and it would fall free. Hank was just a little taller than she was, so if she turned just right —.

"What the! You bitch!" Hank bent over in pain, as Angela's quick swivel and sidekick to his groin caught him off guard. Unfortunately, for Angela, however, the knot didn't come free and she was still loosely roped to Hank.

She yanked on the rope hoping to either pull free or at best, pull Hank to the ground where she could kick him again. It wouldn't give. She took a step forward and kicked at Hank's head, but this time he was ready for her and grabbed her foot and jerked. Down she went with a splash, her head narrowly missing a large rock that protruded from the water. She grabbed at his leg, but he kicked her with the other, sending her backwards and pulling him on top of her. They were now just a foot from the edge of the tailings' pile. He used his free hand to take hold of her throat.

"Oh no, you're not going to escape me that easily." He kept squeezing.

Angela's last thought was, *I guess this is it.* It wasn't.

Hank slowly let up and Angela gasped in some needed air.

"You'll pay for that kick later. For now, you're coming with me." He pulled her up and pushed her ahead of him into the dark, foreboding opening of the mine.

Darkness comes early in the Olympic Mountains, so instead of making it all the way to Tull Canyon, Ray and Kyle were forced to camp for the night several miles north of Buckhorn Lake. Ray was sorry that yesterday he hadn't suggested to Kyle that he be picked up by the helicopter. This day, the low clouds negated that choice and their hiking pace had slowed considerably. He studied his map and figured with an early start, they should get to the old Tull City site around ten.

Bill and his crew were in the same boat. The road closure delay put them at the trailhead off Forest Service Road 2860 too late to start hiking in. They would set out at first light, leaving Sergeant Casper and Pete at the trailhead with one of the radios.

The Shrine

Angela could barely see where she was going as Hank led her down the tunnel. The flashlight provided scant enough light and once they made the first turn the daylight was gone. They'd taken two more right hand turns before entering what at first she thought was another side tunnel, but in fact was a large room carved out of the rock.

"Just stand still." It was more of a command than a suggestion. The rope slackened and then went taut as he moved in the darkness near her. Then, suddenly, there was light.

"That's more like it!" He set the now glowing lantern down. "What do you think?"

The room was huge, rectangular in shape and much greater in area than Bill's cave. At first glance it appeared devoid of any furnishings, but as her eyes adjusted to the dim light, Angela noticed a cot, a small table, a large box and two chairs. The floor was dry, unlike the surface of the main tunnel.

Turning she saw something that made her gasp. It dominated one whole side of the cave.

A large wooden cross was suspended from a rock niche and hung directly over what looked to be a wooden casket. In front of the casket stood a makeshift wooden candelabra, on either side a single candle and on top of the casket, a picture of a man. Nudging her along, Hank walked over to the pile of rocks supporting the casket and lit the three candles.

"You're the first that's ever been here," he said, stepping back. "This is daddy's special place and he's been waiting for you and I."

Angela trembled. *Good God.*

"First things, first, though." Hank led her to the opposite wall and tied her to one of the cot's legs. "This will have to do. Don't try anything stupid again. I'm the only one that knows how to get out of here. Just sit and relax for a while."

As Angela watched silently, horrified of what was to come, Hank unloaded the backpacks and removed the top of the box. From the box, he took out several containers, two gallon-sized milk cartons and single burner propane stove. Then, using a pile of tree limbs she had not noticed, he erected a wall over the opening to the cave room. Satisfied that he had blocked the entrance, he turned to Angela. "There, now that's cozy, if I do say so."

As Angela watched Hank fill two cups from one of the cartons, she racked her brain to think of any way to escape. He handed her one of the cups.

"Here, have some water."

"I'm hungry."

He handed her an energy bar. "That's all you get before the ceremony."

While she ate, Hank rolled out one of the sleeping bags and laid it in front of the shrine. He took the picture and turned to face her.

"If you haven't guessed, this is my father, my daddy."

"I thought he was in jail."

"Oh, that's my step-dad. This is my real daddy. The one in the pen is a real asshole, but this one," now pointing to the coffin, "is the real McCoy, blood of my blood, my hell on earth."

As he spoke, Hank's voice rose in volume and near the end, he was screaming. Angela trembled.

"Okay. Time to show old daddy here that he was wrong."

Hank knelt down, untied Angela from the cot leg and pulled her up.

"Over on the sleeping bag!"

She looked about the cave for anything that could be used to defend herself – *nothing. The candelabra. Maybe.*

"Lie down and pull off your jeans and take off your shirt."

As she did what she was told, Hank stood above her slowly removing his own shirt, shoes and pants.

"Now the bra."

When she didn't respond, he placed his foot on her chest and pressed hard. "Do it!"

While she unhooked the bra she watched in horror as Hank, now naked, began stroking himself. She turned away.

"Now the panties and then roll over on your stomach."

C'mon Angela, do it. When she started to turn, Hank knelt down behind her, but instead of going completely over, Angela grabbed the base of the candelabra and pulled it down. It missed his head, but hit his shoulder.

"Damn. You bitch!"

Angela rolled the other way and dashed toward the wall of branches blocking the entrance. *Maybe, just maybe,* she thought.

Hank was at first slow to react, but quickly recovered and raced after her. "Oh no you don't," he shouted.

Instead of stopping to find a weak spot, Angela ran straight at the center of the wall. *Well here goes,* and then she was through, out into the darkness. Alone.

She could hear Hank screaming behind her, but ran as fast as she could down the tunnel.

"You'll never make it. You'll never get out. I'll find you."

As she ran, she tried to recall what direction and how many turns they'd taken from the cave entrance. She looked back and saw a beam of light. *Hank!*

The map indicated they had about three miles until they reached the B-17 crash site in Tull Canyon. It looked like the trail they were on turned left, skirted around the face of Iron Mountain, above Tubal Cain, and descended into Tull Canyon.

For a half-hour, they'd slowly climbed through a stand of sub-alpine firs, but now the trail was descending again through a swampy area surrounded by large boulders. After a good rest, Kyle seemed in good spirits and they were making better time.

Ray was convinced that Hank's destination was the plane wreckage. Why, he couldn't imagine, but everything pointed to that conclusion. He saw ahead that the trail continued through an open, meadow-like area. He stopped.

"Listen, from now on we need to be as quiet as possible. Right now we're exposed, and in a mile or so we'll be in the canyon. Hank could be anywhere."

"Should we get off the trail?" Kyle asked.

"That's not a bad idea. Let's continue on until we get to that bunch of trees and then we should be able to see down into the canyon," Ray said, pointing ahead toward a stand of firs.

Bill, Lan Thi, Sheriff Wilcox, and one of his deputies, Sam Larson, had been on the trail about two hours, since leaving camp at Silver Creek. They had just branched off the Tubal Cain Trail and picked up the trail to Tull Canyon.

"Look, there's a mine entrance," said Lan Thi, pointing to a dark opening at the base of a cliff that rose above them, just thirty feet up the trail.

"Yeah," said Bill. "That's just one of the many miner's tunnels around here. The Tubal Cain mine entrance is much larger."

The grade was now steeper, winding through a glade of spindly firs and hemlocks. Their pace slowed. Then, just when Wilcox thought he couldn't take another step, the trail leveled off and they entered a swampy area that fronted a picturesque valley. There ahead of them loomed the wreckage of the B-17.

"The tail section and fuselage are behind that stand of trees," Bill said.

"I hope you're right about this and we're in time." Wilcox said.

Bill held his finger to his mouth. "Quiet now."

The wreckage was strewn across the landscape, much covered by years of ground vegetation growth and hidden in dense clusters of willow trees. What remained of the fuselage and the tail, with its identification number 746 still readable, were two of the larger pieces. It was not surprising that so many small pieces were so widely scattered. The plane had actually hit the ridge 2000 feet above and then slid like a giant cigar down the precipitous slope.

"He could be anyplace watching us approach," Bill continued.

"I'd think he would be in the fuselage," said Wilcox, crouching next to Bill and Lan.

"Let's split up. Bill, you and Lan go around to the right, the rest of us will circle around to the left, over where the tail is," Wilcox pointed.

Bill quickly stuck out his hand. "Wait, get down," he whispered. "I see something moving up behind the tail section."

They watched as two figures moved stealthily down the canyon to the right of the tail section. Lan nudged Bill.

"That looks like Ray and Deputy Peterson," she said.

"Are you sure," Wilcox said, now raising up to get a better view.

"It is them," Bill said. "Your eyes are better than mine."

"Now what?" Wilcox asked.

"We shouldn't shout. I'll stand up and wave my arm," Bill said. At first he got no indication that they saw him, but then Ray stopped and waved his arm in response.

―――

They'd already searched the hillside near the tail section and had doubled back to approach the fuselage. Ray was convinced now they had to be in that large section. As he and Kyle neared the cockpit end, Ray spotted Bill waving his arm.

"Looks like we got here before them," Kyle said.

"Yeah." *Now what?* he thought. He waved to Bill and by sign language tried to indicate that they would approach the fuselage from their end and for Bill's team to come up from his side. By Bill's gestures and nods, it looked like he understood.

A few minutes later they had their answer. The fuselage was empty of any humans, only pieces of tangled metal and wiring.

They somberly greeted one another.

"Any ideas?" Ray didn't ask anyone in particular.

"Not a clue," Bill said. "We do know for sure that he was on the Hoh Lake Trail and everything else points to him coming here."

"Sheriff?"

Wilcox shook his head.

Just then, Sergeant Casper's voice came over Wilcox's radio.

"Can't hear you very good," Wilcox said. "I'll get to higher ground." He started climbing up the hill behind the plane wreckage, all the time trying to keep in contact. Ray and the others watched as Wilcox climbed higher.

In a few minutes he descended and walked over to the group.

"I think I know where he might be. Casper just got some very interesting information about Mr. Hank Mason from his office. You'll never believe this!"

Into the Light

~~~

Angela shivered and forced herself as far back as possible, unsure where she was. After several stumbles, she'd fallen down, and searching for the wall to right herself, felt the opening and crawled in. Hank passed by seconds later, the beam of his flashlight visible from the recess.

The rough edges of her hiding place rubbed against her. Listening for any sign of Hank, she tried straightening up, but found no room to, and ended up scraping herself. *I've got to get out of here*, she told herself, but she stayed still. Several minutes passed.

Angela listened again. Nothing. She crouched down and eased herself out. *Now what?* Trying to remember which way she'd run, Angela turned left and slowly felt her way down the tunnel. She stopped abruptly. *What was that? Hank coming back?* She picked up her pace and then suddenly she saw light.

It was the entrance to the shrine room! Quickly she stepped through the branches. Hank was not there. Angela's mind raced trying to think where she could hide. She grabbed her shirt, which still lay near the casket, hoping Hank would not notice its absence.

"Angela, Angela." It was Hank. He was shouting at the top of his lungs. "Angela, where are you?"

After descending from Tull Canyon and hiking southwest on the main trail, they crossed Copper Creek and entered the meadow area that had been the site of Tubal Cain Camp. Above them, some 400 feet up the hill of ore tailings, lay the entrance to Tubal Cain Mine.

Ray and Bill started up the precipitous grade, with Deputies Kyle Peterson and Sam Larson behind them. Lan Thi and Sheriff Wilcox stayed below. Half way up, Ray stopped cold in his tracks. "Did you hear that?"

"Yes. Sounded like someone yelling Angela," Bill said.

Even though it was hard to believe what he'd just learned about Hank, Ray didn't argue with Wilcox's logic and like everyone else, had quickly headed to the Tubal Cain Mine. Now the sound of Hank's screaming voice confirmed they had been right and also that Angela was still alive.

"C'mon, let's go, another couple of minutes and we'll be there."

"Slow down, Ray, you just can't charge in there. There are miles of passageways," Bill said.

"I realize that, but if we heard his voice, he can't be too far in," Ray answered.

They crested the tailings' pile and the mine entrance came into view.

"I'm going in!"

Bill grabbed him. "Okay, but let's take it easy and ..."

He pulled away and ran for the entrance. Bill, was right behind.

Ray stopped short of the entrance and yelled, "Angela!" He yelled again. No answer.

―――

Both Angela and Hank heard Ray's call. Hank had backtracked and was just about to reenter his special room. Angela was crouched low behind the casket.

Her first reaction was to shout back, but not knowing where Hank was, she lay still.

Hank quickly decided he had two choices. Go into the cave room and extinguish the lights and hope they wouldn't find his lair, or retreat back into the mine. The sound of approaching feet and lights made up his mind. He turned around and disappeared into the waiting darkness.

Angela heard the sound of someone pushing aside the wall of branches. *Wait. Was that Bill's voice?*

"Oh my God, will you look at all this," Bill said.

"Ray, you've got good eyes. If you hadn't seen that light, we'd have turned the other way, for sure," Kyle said.

"Ray, what's wrong?"

They turned to follow Ray's gaze. He was staring at the casket and at the slowly emerging shape. "Angela!"

"Yes, it's me, in the flesh, literally. Throw me my jeans."

A minute later, Angela walked from behind the shrine, into Ray's waiting arms.

Deputy Peterson let the young couple have their moment, before asking the question on all their minds. "Where's Hank Mason?"

"I don't know. He was chasing me when I found a place to hide. Could have been ten, fifteen minutes ago. I'm not sure."

"We heard him yell and no one's come out, so he must still be in here," Kyle said. "Sam, you stay here while the rest of us go outside. I'm sure Lan will be happy to see you Angela."

"Lan's okay then? Oh, thank God. I thought sure he'd hurt her."

"She's waiting down below," Bill said.

"I need a minute." She picked up the rest of her belongings and turned to Bill. "By the way, how did you find me?"

"That's a long story, as the saying goes, but one you'll find fascinating," Bill said.

"Okay, I'm really ready to get out of here," Angela said.

No one asked Angela one of the obvious questions, but Peterson figured that could wait.

When the room they were in had been carved out for a storage area during the mine's peak years, an air duct had been drilled from the ceiling out to the main tunnel. The diameter was easily three feet and it was in here that Hank had crawled and been able to watch them and listen to their conversation.

What fools they are, he thought. *I'm still in control. I'll wait till the others have gone and then make my move.*

Slowly he inched back down the air duct until he reached the floor of the tunnel. Then it began to dawn on him that there was only one way out. They didn't have to search for him, they could just wait him out. He needed a plan. *Think!*

The two women clung together as if they'd never expected to see each other again. Tears streamed down Lan's face and when Angela started to say something, she sobbed and added her own contribution to the flow. They realized how different their fates could have been.

Wilcox turned to the men. "Okay. The women are safe and now what do we do about Mason?"

"There are so many side tunnels and probably small caves that he could be anywhere," Bill said.

"I think I'll have Kyle and Sam stay here, not inside that room, but outside and then eventually he'll have to come out or starve," Wilcox said.

The women caught the tail end of the conversation and Angela reached out for Ray's hand. "Listen, before we do anything, would someone tell me how you found me and what's the story on that room with the casket?"

"I'll let Ray tell you Angela while we get back to the road. I'm going to give as much food and water as we have to Kyle and Sam, then we should get started."

They said goodbye to the deputies as they climbed back up the tailings' pile, and then headed down Tubal Cain Trail.

"Okay, Ray, let's hear it," Angela said.

"Before I tell you, you tell me about your time with Hank."

"Ray, c'mon, I'm okay. Nothing happened … he didn't get to …ah … I'll tell you later. Please?"

He stopped and pulled her into his arms. "All right."

Ray told her what Sergeant Casper had learned about Hank and his parents and what had happened on Hank's thirteenth birthday.

Hank's dad, his biological father, disappeared mysteriously on a backpacking trip with Hank in 1972.

Casper found out that when Hank was a child, he was not only of small stature, but slightly built and constantly fussed over by his doting mother. When his dad traveled out of town, Hank slept with his mother and continued to, well after his twelfth birthday. Hank's dad constantly accused him of being a "little girl" and harped on him for not playing sports and for being a "momma's boy." By the time Hank reached puberty his dad's harangues increased, especially when his son still seemed to enjoy, as his dad called them, "pansy things."

In the summer of 1972, Hank's dad decided to take him on an overnight hike in Tull Canyon. He told his wife, "it will make a man out of him." His father was very punctual and when they were one day late, Hank's concerned mother called the sheriff's office, who in turn contacted the Park Service.

The morning of the second day of the search, they found Hank curled up asleep in the fuselage of the crashed B-17. At first he was incoherent, then slowly he told how on their second day of hiking, his dad decided to explore the Tubal Cain mine. Impatient with Hank's reluctance to go into the mine, his dad called him a coward and told him to stay at the entrance while he looked around. Hank said that was the last he saw of his dad.

Several members of the search team explored the mine for hours, but never found any trace of Hank's dad. Everyone's best guess was that he fell into some unknown crevasse. Some, however, speculated he found another way out and deserted Hank, perhaps to frighten the boy. But then, where was he? Had he planned all along to run away from his family? The newspapers and wire services ran speculative stories for days.

After Hank's return home, another team of Park Rangers and volunteers searched the mine, but when one of the team got lost for an hour, they discontinued the effort.

"So that's probably Hank's dad in the casket?"

"Your guess is as good as mine, Angela," said Ray. "It sure looks like a burial site."

"How would he get a casket up here?" Angela asked.

Voices from the Mountain

"Probably made it with wood from the old Tull City and Tubal Cain Camp ruins, I'd guess," added Bill. "Wilcox and some Park Service people are coming back tomorrow. Then we'll know for sure what's under that pile of rocks or in the casket."

"Hank never talked about any of this?" Angela asked Ray.

"No. Everything we knew about him started with his years in high school. He must have taken his step-father's name."

"Mason, you mean?"

"Yes. Hank's dad's name was Winchester, Henry Winchester."

―――§―――

Hank had crawled back into the air duct, but when the sheriff came and got the two men, he made his way back down to the floor of the mine tunnel. Now he was just a few feet away from the entrance to the room. He wasn't positive anyone was there, so he cautiously peeked around the corner, scanned the room and crossed the threshold. Using his flashlight, he silently crossed to the storage box and removed what he needed for his escape.

―――§―――

Dead End

He used his Zippo lighter to ignite one of the candles. Then, kneeling down, he placed the candle under the edge of the casket. Next he gathered the branches he'd used to block the entrance and stacked them on the other side of the casket, directly under the cross. Stepping back, he lit the pile. *That should do it*, he thought. *So long daddy!*

The branches were dry and instantaneously the pile became a raging inferno and smoke quickly billowed towards the ceiling. The flames from the candle and the nearby burning branches licked at the casket and it too began to be consumed. Before Hank realized what was happening, smoke filled the room and he couldn't see the entrance. He picked up his pack and strode in the direction he thought led to the way out.

He found the opening and turned right, all the time gasping for breath. Two more turns and he'd be at the mine entrance, then he'd deal with that idiot deputy. He felt in his pack for the revolver that had once been his dad's. It had come in handy once before. *Wait ... I should have gone to the left.*

The smoke was now beginning to fill the tunnel and Hank's flashlight was useless. *Got to go back.* He crashed into the wall of the tunnel. "Damn!" *Keep going you dummy!* There was an air duct he'd never explored. *Maybe, just maybe.*

Kyle was the first to notice the smoke emanating from the cave.

"Jeez! Sam, look."

"What should we do?"

"I don't know about you, but I'm not going in there."

"See if you can get Wilcox on the radio," Sam said.

On the second try, Kyle made contact. "Yes, it's pouring out. Okay. All right, I'll call you back."

"What did he say?"

"Just what we thought. Wait it out. When the smoke stops, go in and take a look."

"Figure Mason set the fire?"

"Probably, but why trap yourself?"

"Shit, I don't know. What a mess."

Last Session

Dr. Schlossburg had been listening for almost an hour. Ray stood up and walked to the window. There were whitecaps moving southwest to northeast across Elliot Bay and one of the Yakima class ferries looked to be struggling to reach its mooring at Coleman Dock. In the distance, dark clouds hung over The Brothers Mountain on the Olympic Peninsula.

"Looks a little stormy for early September."

"Yes, a bit." Schlossburg swiveled around in his chair. "So that's it. They never found Hank?"

"Nope." Ray returned to the chair facing Schlossburg's desk. "Not a trace."

"When's the big wedding?"

"Next Saturday."

"Ray, I know you think this thing with Hank is all over, but it's going to be with you and Angela for a long time. I'd like to put you under just one more time. There's still a missing link here and there and it might help."

Voices from the Mountain

Ray shook his head. "I don't know, I...?"

"C'mon, it can't do any harm. Besides, the Seattle Police Department paid for this many sessions.

"Okay." Ray was still hesitant.

"I still think there are several unresolved issues."

"All right, but I've got to meet Angela, Bill and Lan at Fredrick's at two, so let's get it over with."

Schlossburg reached in his desk drawer and pulled out the pendant. Ray knew the routine and relaxed.

"Ray, I want to go back to your hike three years ago." He slowly swung the pendant. "The hike with Pete, Larry and Gordy. You're hiking up the Dosewallips Trail to Anderson Pass -----."

The moon barely gives me enough light to make my way to the edge to take a pee. Stupid not to bring the flashlight. What's that? Someone's behind me. River water splashing. The noise again. An animal? Someone coming out from behind the tree. Moonlight. Shadow of a tall – Tall, that can't be --- The blow – darkness –no, no ------. Darkness!

"Ray, Ray, that's it, you're okay. Ray wake up." Schlossburg clapped his hands.

"That was weird," Ray said, opening his eyes and stretching. "I remembered that the person who hit me was tall, about my height, but that can't be."

"Maybe you confused that image with something that occurred when you were with Bill at Anderson Pass. When you heard the voices."

"Could be, but the memory was so vivid. Then I remembered the blow and, well, that did it for me."

Schlossburg turned and reached in the bookcase behind him. "Here, these are for you."

"My journals from the cave."

"Yes. They were helpful, but they're yours. Who knows, you may write a book about your adventures some day." He paused. "You know, Ray, I've always been bothered by one thing in this whole scenario. Something that just doesn't ring true."

"What's that?"

"How Hank Mason could have followed you all that way and been there that night at Anderson Pass Camp."

Double Ring

Lake Quinault glistened in the setting sun and a cool breeze from the north heralded the changing of seasons while lightly rustling the purple bows and ribbons on the arbor. In an hour the two couples would exchange vows beneath the arbor, surrounded by their guests seated in rows of chairs arranged in a semicircle on the freshly mown lawn that gently sloped to the lake from the Lodge porch.

Angela and Lan were going over final details for the meal with the social manager, while the staff at Lake Quinault Lodge was busily preparing the banquet room for the reception that would follow the wedding.

The choice of Lake Quinault Lodge for their weddings had seemed appropriate; it was after all, central to most of what had happened in their lives the past three years. Angela asked two close friends from college to be her bridesmaids, Lan asked her cousin from Portland. Ray asked Pete, Larry and Gordy to be the groomsmen. They didn't have an official best man or maid of honor; rather they elected to have each other fill that role for the opposite couple. Edie Cox from the Mercantile was in charge of the reception.

Ray invited Sergeant Casper and Dr. Schlossburg to attend, but both declined. Deputy Kyle Peterson and Sheriff Wilcox did accept, as did Angela's friend Ranger Jerry Helspath from Kalaloch.

The double ring ceremony went off without a hitch and after some photographs on the lawn, everyone followed the brides and grooms into the Lodge's banquet room for the reception.

"Great wedding, Ray, Angela," said Sheriff Wilcox, as he passed through the reception line. "It wasn't that long ago that I would never have imaged you two being here together." Then he shook Bill's hand. "You too, Bill and Lan. I'm sure happy it's all turned out this way."

Bill returned the shake. "That's for sure." Then leaning toward Wilcox, "When you have a moment later, I'd like to talk to you about something."

As the evening wore on, the bridal party and the guests enjoyed an ample supply of good wine and beer, so by the time the band arrived, everyone was "party hearty."

After Bill got the band set up, he looked for Wilcox and found him outside on the porch. "Getting chilly, Sheriff."

"Yes, it is. Winter's just around the corner. You had a question for me?"

""I was curious about anything new on Hank Mason, but didn't want to bring it up earlier."

"No, that's okay. Actually, we've just about declared the case closed as far as Jefferson County is concerned. I talked to Casper in Seattle and they are close to calling it quits, too. The problem is, there's no real hard evidence that Hank died in the cave fire. Everything in the room where the fire started was completely consumed. We were able to find a few bone fragments, but these could have been his dad's from the casket."

"So you think for sure that his missing father's body was in the casket?"

"From what Angela told us and what we saw before the fire, I'd say for sure."

"Do you think Hank killed him?"

"We'll never be positive." He looked over Bill's shoulder. "Here comes Ray."

"Hi Bill, Sheriff. Say, have you seen Angela?"

"She and Lan went to change about forty minutes ago," Bill answered. "I just saw Lan before I came out here."

"Yes, Lan's back, but Angela isn't. They were supposed to meet in front of the fireplace fifteen minutes ago," Ray said.

Wilcox poked Bill lightly in the ribs. "Probably nervous about tonight." Wilcox laughed at his little joke.

"No, seriously you guys, she's never late and I already went to our room and she's not there."

Just then they heard screams coming from the direction of the banquet room and then a loud bang!

Wilcox reacted first. "My God, that sounded like a gunshot." Not waiting for an answer, he ran through the French doors and headed towards the banquet room, with Bill and Ray right behind him.

The sight that greeted them was one of mass disarray, but it was what he saw on the bandstand that caused Ray's whole being to shake with fear and trepidation. Everywhere the guests were cowered on the floor or crouching behind their chairs, focused on the two people on the bandstand.

Hank Mason held a revolver in one hand and the other was holding tight to a rope cinched around Angela's neck.

"Welcome to the party, Ray!" he screamed as they rushed in. "My, what a lovely bride you have here. I'm hurt that I wasn't on the guest list."

Hank's face had the evilest look Ray had ever seen. It instantly reminded him of the Jack Nicholson character in "The Shining." His clothes were in tatters and he had an ugly scar that ran from his left ear to his chin.

"Just thought I'd give you one more look before we sail away." He pointed the gun at Larry. "And you, big fellow, you're with us. I need an able-bodied seaman."

Larry didn't move. Hank fired a shot, just missing Larry's leg and hitting a nearby table. "Move! The rest of you stay on the floor and you Ray, just get out of my way."

Larry backed towards the door as Hank stepped down from the riser, and holding the gun to Angela's neck, followed. As he passed, Bill was tempted to make a grab for him, but Hank glared at Bill as if to say, "just try it."

Wilcox watched helplessly as Hank pulled Angela into the lobby, past the fireplace and out onto the porch where he'd been joking with Ray just a few minutes earlier. Larry was walking a few paces in front of Hank and apparently being told where to go.

Bill, Wilcox and Ray followed at a safe distance, not wanting to rile Hank, but frustrated that he had the upper hand. Bill broke their silence.

"Looks like he's heading to the pier."

Lady on the Lake

They watched in helpless exasperation as Larry stepped into the boat and sat next to the motor. He held the boat fast while Hank untied the mooring line and guided Angela onto the center seat, before climbing in next to her. Larry started the motor, pulled away and headed towards the north shore.

Wilcox, who was already on the phone to his office, let them know where Hank seemed to be going and told them to set up road blocks on the north shore road.

Those watching in the fading light from the Lodge lawn let out a unison gasp as they saw Larry suddenly stand. He had his arm around Hank's head and was pulling him up from the seat. As Hank reacted, he dropped Angela's rope and his gun. In an instant, Larry jumped out of the boat, taking Hank with him.

Hank was no match for Larry and he swiftly pulled him under. As this was going on, Ray yelled to Angela to grab the rudder arm of the boat, which was still motoring on its course.

Larry's head appeared, then his arm, still locked around Hank who, despite his physical disadvantage was putting up a good fight. They went under again. When Larry reappeared, his arms were empty.

Angela brought the boat around and slowly came up next to Larry, who grabbed hold of the side and held on as Angela pointed the bow back to the south shore and the Lodge's pier.

Bill grabbed the bow as Ray took Angela's hand, lifted her out and took her in his arms.

"Thank God you're okay."

"Thanks to Larry!" she said.

As Lan rushed up to them, Ray let Angela go and helped Bill pull out Larry. He was sopping wet and splashed water all over them.

"Sorry 'bout that Ray."

"Don't worry about it. I owe you a lot. Let's get you dry."

Wilcox was already climbing into the boat. "I'm going out to check before it's too dark, but it sure looked from here like we're finally rid of Hank Mason, thanks to you, Larry."

"I tried to swim in with him when he stopped struggling, but I lost him. It was hard to see under water and I was out of breath."

"Don't worry about it, Larry, you did what you had to do to save Angela and probably yourself," Wilcox said. "I'll be back shortly and we can talk about it some more. Consider yourself a hero."

Pete, Gordy, Ray and Larry walked arm-in-arm back to the Lodge. "Just like old times, huh Larry, the Motley Crew triumphs against all odds."

"C'mon guys I only did what any of you would have done," Larry said.

Voices

The excitement of the evening's rescue was enough for most of the guests. The few that remained sat in front of the lobby fireplace drinking wine. Before Sheriff Wilcox left he told the Lodge staff that he would be back in the morning with divers.

By eleven Bill and Lan went to their room in the Lodge Annex, leaving only Ray, Angela, Pete and Larry to watch the last of the embers die out.

"Betty's already upstairs, so I'm heading up too," said Pete. "Congratulations again you two. This has been quite a night."

"See you in the morning Pete," said Angela. She looked at Ray, who seemed to be half asleep. "Ray, Pete's leaving."

"Oh, sorry Pete. Yes, see you in the morn."

Pete turned to Angela with a broad grin on his face. "Gee, if he's this out of it, Angela, it won't be much of a beginning to your honeymoon."

"C'mon, Pete, I was just thinking of something. Don't worry about me, I'll be just fine!"

Angela rose from her chair, smiled and gave Ray a kiss.

"Don't be too long, sweetheart. Goodnight Larry and thanks again."

"I'm beat, also. See you tomorrow, Ray," Larry said, glancing at Ray and following Angela up the stairs.

Ray took a final sip of his wine. He hadn't just been daydreaming or dozing off. Something was bothering him. It was something he'd heard today that reminded him of the time he was at Anderson Pass and had heard voices. What was it?

It will keep. Time to join my new wife.

In the early morning hours it came to him. *Son of a bitch!*

He left his sleeping bride and went down to the lobby, which was filling up with guests waiting for the restaurant to open. He bought a coffee at the breakfast bar and went out on the porch. It was as if he was waiting for him and Ray strode right up to face him.

"It was you, wasn't it? Not Hank."

"Yes. How …?"

"It was when you got water on me and said, 'sorry 'bout that Ray'." He looked straight into Larry's eyes. "I remembered the last time I'd heard that – at night at Anderson Pass Camp."

Larry slowly walked to the railing and then down the steps to the lawn. "It's a long story, but I guess …"

"Guess what? For Christ's sake, why in hell did you hit me that night? Everyone, including the cops, thinks it was Hank."

Larry stopped at the gazebo and turned. His eyes were filled with tears and the big man trembled uncontrollably.

"It was either do what Hank wanted or give up my chance of ever playing ball again or having a chance at turning pro."

"What? I don't get it."

"Hank was convinced you would eventually remember seeing him in the hallway when he raped Donna Jones."

"So you didn't have anything to do with any of the rapes?"
"No!"
"But why in hell would you try to kill me to protect Hank?" Ray shook his head.
"Hank found something out about me when we were freshman and he threatened to tell everyone. It would have ruined me."
"So bad that you'd kill someone?"
"Ray, Hank found me with another guy."
"What do you mean, 'found'?"
"On winter break." Larry paused, then slowly, "On the third floor. In bed."
"You and another guy?"
"Yes. He's been blackmailing me all these years."
"So, it wasn't by accident that Hank picked you to take him away in the boat?"
Larry shook his head.

Autumn often arrives early in the Enchanted Valley and this year was no exception. Though dominated by evergreens, there are enough deciduous plants and trees to add color to the landscape that greeted late season hikers.

Such a scene welcomed both sets of newlyweds. For each of the couples, spending a few days in the Valley together was an appropriate end to their wedding festivities. They weren't calling it a honeymoon. That would come later when they had the money and time. To Ray, Angela and Bill it was only fitting that they revisit the forest and mountains that held so many memories for them and where events were set in motion that would shape their lives for years to come.

For Lan too, being in the mountains took her back to those days in Viet Nam when she had been with her family and Bill.

They set up their tents at the edge of the Quinault River within walking distance of the chalet and in a spot where they had an unencumbered view of the snow-covered peaks that surrounded them.

"The beauty of this Valley always takes my breath away," said Angela. "I'll never tire of coming here."

"Nor will I," Ray said, taking his wife's hand.

Angela squeezed his hand and smiled. "At least I won't have a mother bear after me tonight."

"What's that?" Lan said.

"Oh, that's another story. I'll tell you about it sometime."

"C'mon you two," Bill said. "If you want Saturday night dinner, we'd better get a fire going."

"Speaking of Saturday night, Ray, isn't Larry starting the game tomorrow for the Seahawks?" Angela asked.

"Yes, he is. We'll have other times to see him play."

"I'll never be able to thank him enough for saving me."

Ray bent to light the fire. "Oh, I think he knows how much we appreciate what he did."

"One of your voices tell you that?" Bill said.

"In a way. Hey, what's for dinner? I'm starved."

Bill turned, reached deep into his pack and spun around with a flourish, holding a can in front of himself.

"What else! Baked beans, your favorite, remember?"